Black Bra and Panties

Also by Reggie Chesterfield:
Turned Out!

Reggie Chesterfield

Black Bra and Panties

New Tradition Books

Black Bra and Panties

New Tradition Books
ISBN 1932420118

*This book is a work of fiction. Names, characters, places
and incidents are either the product of the author's
imagination or are used fictitiously. Any resemblance to
actual events or locales or persons, living or dead is
entirely coincidental.*

For information contact:
New Tradition Books
newtraditionbooks@yahoo.com

1

Josie stepped out of the airport and into the bright California sunlight.

It felt so good to be back.

She adjusted the hem of her short skirt as she walked to the taxi stand. It seemed that it was always riding up and partially showing her bottom. It wasn't that she minded anyone seeing her bottom. It was just that it was a little uncomfortable. The way she looked at it, either she was wearing a skirt or she wasn't. If it kept riding it up, she would definitely have to just take it off. The only problem was that she wasn't wearing any panties. She didn't mind anyone seeing her like that either. She just didn't want to get arrested. She attracted attention with her gorgeous looks and dark red hair, but sometimes attention wasn't always a good thing. She had been arrested once before for public lewdness at a Lakers game, so she didn't want to go there again. She had been told by some unreliable sources that if she flashed the TV camera, it would boost her career in the adult industry. Of course, it hadn't. Her footage was never shown and all she ended up with was a fine.

Regardless, it was good to be back in Los Angeles. She had just spent a boring week at her parents' place back east and was ready to get back into the swing of things. It had been nice to visit home, and while she had felt great about being there, she felt even better about leaving. Of course, her parents had been all hung up about her career choice, even though they had always told her to "follow her dream." She couldn't help it that her dream just happened to be in porn.

While she had always been sexually promiscuous, it was only after her college roommate, Julie, had helped to turn her out that she realized that she wanted to be a porno actress. It was the first time she had been home since she had started making movies. The parental units were *not* very happy. Unlike most of the girls who hid their on-screen sexual activities from their parents, she had never had any hesitation about telling them. They had always said they would love her "no matter what." And they did, but they couldn't help but foster a bit of the typical parental judgmental behavior. They were such hypocrites, she thought. Her dad, Hal, was a motivational speaker and self-help guru. He was initially afraid that it would hurt his business, but had only reluctantly admitted that since she started screwing on film, his business had increased by forty-six percent.

He had said, "Josie, I know that you think it's cool and everything, but don't you ever think about where you'll be in five years?"

"Yes, Daddy, I have. I think that I'll still be in California making porno."

He shook his head. "What I'm saying, dear, is do you think that you'll want to do something else? Like maybe work in sales or be a nurse. Or even a lawyer."

She thought about this for a second. "I don't know. I mean, why would I want to do stuff like that? It's not like what I do is hard work or anything plus I make really good money."

Her father threw up his hands in desperation.

Her mother, Priscilla, a gorgeous middle aged woman, was a little more receptive about her career choice.

"So, do you get to have threesomes and everything?" Priscilla asked.

Josie couldn't help but blush. "Mom! I can't believe you just asked me that!"

"C'mon. I just want to be supportive. So, do you get to have group sex?"

Josie rolled her eyes. "Yes, Mom. I get to have group sex. I basically do whatever it is they want me to do and if that includes group sex, I do it."

Mom leaned in close and looked over her shoulder to see if Dad was listening. He wasn't. He was busy trying to fix a clasp on Josie's bracelet. It had broken on the flight over.

"So, do a lot of the fellows have really big...you know?" Priscilla held out her hands to emphasize.

Josie blushed again. "Mom!"

"Tell me. I bet you really get it good, don't you?"

Josie sighed and smiled. She couldn't believe that her mom was being so cool with this. "Well, most of them are pretty big. But this one black guy had a dick that was..." Josie used her hands to illustrate a penis that was around ten inches long.

Her mom gasped in amazement.

"I'm so happy for you, honey. Doing what you want like this. I just wish I had had the guts to do what you do at your age. I mean it's taken me years..."

Before she could finish, Dad loudly cleared his throat and gave her a look.

She stopped what she was saying and quickly changed her tone. "Oh...I'm sorry. I'm happy that you're happy, but you really need to be careful. I would hate for you to be hurt."

Josie thought that it was a little odd that her mom had changed the subject like that, but thought no more of it. She spent the rest of her week hanging out at the house and seeing her old high school friends. Most of them were now either married or fat. These were the ones that hadn't gone away to college like her. Some of them were a little shocked at her career, but most seemed envious. Especially the male ones. They thought that it was amazing that she got paid to have sex on film. Josie didn't really pay them too much attention though, because they were all dumpy and had beerbellies.

Yes, it was boring. It hadn't been hard for her to come back to California.

The taxi pulled up at her apartment and she paid the cabbie and went in.

Her roommate, Marcy, was sitting on the sofa watching television. She was also a porno actress and was built like a brick shithouse. She had definitely gotten her money's worth when she had gotten her breast implants. Josie was still on the fence as far as breast augmentation went. Her fans begged her not to, but it seemed as though the industry people wanted her to do it. She just didn't know what to do so she did nothing. She thought she had pretty good tits. She had never had any complaints about her C-cups.

As soon as she saw Josie, Marcy leaped up and hugged Josie.

"I'm so glad you're back! Did you have a good trip?" She gave Josie a deep open mouthed welcome-home kiss. She and Josie, while not being lesbians or anything, occasionally had sex together when they were bored and horny and didn't feel like going out. They did this stuff in the movies all the time, so why wouldn't they do it in real life, as well?

Josie returned the kiss and ran her hand between Marcy's legs, feeling her pussy lips through her tight black stretch pants.

"I'm glad to be back."

Marcy purred, "I couldn't wait for you to get back."

She began to nuzzle Josie's neck and put her hand up Josie's top, feeling her firm breasts. Josie responded by putting her hand in Marcy's pants. Marcy quickly worked her way down Josie's toned body with her tongue. Once she was on her knees, she pushed Josie's skirt up and began to kiss Josie's pussy. Josie moaned. It was the first time she had had sex since she had left California. She had left immediately after filming an eight man gangbang and had hoped that that would hold her until she got back. It hadn't.

Josie maneuvered Marcy over to the sofa so that the dark haired girl could access her pussy more easily. She loved having sex with Marcy. The girl knew exactly what buttons to push and she couldn't help but writhe and whip her red hair in ecstasy as the dark haired girl worked her pussy into a froth. Marcy worked like madwoman, eating like she was starved. Josie came twice before she couldn't even think about it.

"Are you going to let me have a taste?" She said breathlessly as Marcy continued to lap her up.

"Oh, yeah!" Marcy grinned as she looked up from between her legs.

Marcy climbed up on the couch and pulled down her pants and let Josie go to work, but not before deeply kissing Josie. Josie loved the taste of herself on Marcy's lips and got even more turned on as she got started. As she licked Marcy's big lips, she fingered herself to another orgasm. Marcy came almost immediately once Josie got started. The girls kept at it for a good hour before they finally were spent.

Laying there half-dressed and smoking cigarettes, Josie's attention wandered between Marcy and the TV.

"So, did your parents get on your nerves?" Marcy asked as she stroked Josie's leg.

"No, not really, just the usual what-am-I doing-with-my-life crap."

"What did you tell them?"

"Nothing much. I mean, what am I gonna say when they ask me what I'm going to be doing in five years when I don't know?" Josie said.

Marcy nodded.

Josie looked down and ashed her cigarette. What would she be doing in five years? Sure, being a porno actress was fine, but what about the other parts of her life? Surely, there was more to her than just sex? She tried to push these serious thoughts out of her head. She turned her attention to the television.

"Who's that?" She said as she looked at a wild looking red haired man preaching fire and brimstone to a bunch of shabbily dressed parishioners. He looked to be in his mid-thirties and sported a big, slicked back pompadour and sideburns. He could have been a rockabilly singer just as easily as he was a fundamentalist preacher. His look gave off the impression that if he hadn't been a preacher he would have probably been in prison. He grinned maniacally as he stalked around the stage. They watched in amazement as he grabbed a slick haired man in an expensive suit from behind the organ. The guy didn't look surprised. In fact, he looked like one of the preacher's right hand men. The preacher then proceeded to remove his own belt and tie it around the hands of the man.

"You've got to throw that devil out! Throw him out!"

With that, he grabbed the man, who was laughing, and threw him off stage. "Get out, Satan! Get out of my church!"

Then he turned to the congregation. "That devil won't be bothering us no more, brothers and sisters." He grinned and wiped his brow.

Then he went back to stalking around the stage and pounding his Bible.

The two girls looked on in amazement.

"I think that's Brother Red Hair," Marcy said. "I think that this show is called, *The Church of What's Happenin' Now.*"

"*What's Happenin' Now*? Man, he looks happenin' to be going crazy," Josie laughed.

"It must be the red hair," Marcy said winking. "You know what they say about those redheads."

Josie stared at her in mock anger.

"I'm gonna get you for that!" With that she pounced on Marcy and the two girls started up again.

2

As he relaxed in his recliner and got blowjob, Brother Leon "Red" Hair smoked a cigarette and realized that he was, by far, the luckiest person he had ever known. And this was saying something, because he had met quite a few people. He had grown up in a little town in Texas, impoverished and with no apparent prospects. Everybody there had considered him to be typical local white trash. They figured he would either end up in a factory or in prison, just like ninety percent of the rest of the town's population.

However, there was one thing that they didn't know about Red. That was the fact that he had dreams. Sure, this didn't make him any different from any of the other assholes who lived in the town. Most of them had dreams too. Their dreams were the typical mundane small town fantasies of being rich, having a nice car, joining the Army or getting married. His was a little more specific.

He had at first wanted to be a science fiction writer. He had an idea for a masterpiece titled, *The Man Who Could Shit Worlds.* He wasn't sure if he would ever be able to put the astounding concepts in his head down on paper but he would try. The book would be about a man who through some amazing mental evolution could actually defecate galaxies. The whole concept of everything in the world being nothing but the waste material of a greater organism was a riveting one for Red. The novel would be mind boggling, but only if he could organize his thoughts enough to write it. It would be his life's crowning achievement. And if that didn't work out, he wanted to be a TV preacher.

Most people just couldn't see that Red was different from all the rest of the losers in town who claimed to have dreams. The difference was that he knew how to make his dream come true. Since he had chronic writers block and had never been able to write the first sentence of his magnum opus, he had opted for the latter dream. The one about being a TV preacher.

He moved the girl's head up and down on his penis with his heavily tattooed arms, a byproduct of a brief rebellious streak in his early twenties. The tattoos were of Biblical scenes such as the burning bush and Judas hanging himself. He sometimes used them as tools to better illustrate his sermons. With their bright colors and amazing detail, they looked absolutely stunning on TV.

One of Red's most important characteristics was that he loved church and he loved to study people. He also hated to see people suffer. Since he had grown up poor, he was always looking for a way to help out the underprivileged. He realized early on that no matter what kind of nonsense passed through the lips of the most religious people in the congregation, it would inevitably be accepted as fact. One of the deacons could come in one day and say something to the order of, "Man didn't walk on the moon. It was all a trick of the devil to make everybody lose sight of God." Sure enough, five minutes later, everybody in the congregation would accept as truth the fact that man didn't walk on the moon, whether they actually believed it or not. They were afraid to say anything in opposition to it for fear of being labeled an atheist.

Red made note of all this and realized that he could pretty much go out there and say anything he wanted. And as long he kept it within the context of religion, he would always be able to find someone to follow him. But moreover, he could use this power to help people. People are always more likely to help others if there is religion involved. He always considered himself a good person and hated to see suffering. It was the perfect mix. Besides, he was good looking and charismatic. That didn't hurt either.

Another thing going for him was the fact that he had always been popular with the girls in church. The funny thing about it was that while he was considered to be a very handsome boy, none of the girls ever really paid any attention to him until one day he started nodding off in church. He had stayed up late the night before watching *The Good, The Bad and the Ugly*, and could barely keep his eyes open. Of course when he started falling asleep, he started to get really relaxed and before long, he had a boner the size of Houston in his pants. He had always considered it a blessing that he was so well-endowed, but still he didn't think he was anything special. After all, eleven inches wasn't that big, was it?

The girls really started eyeing him and making every effort to get him to go home with them. He did, of course, and lost his virginity very quickly. He bedded every girl in his Sunday school class within the month, but only after they had had a private Bible study. He soon came to see his prodigious penis as a divine tool. The sessions kept up pretty regularly and news of the size of his penis eventually got around to the older, married women in the church as well. Soon, he was being invited over for *private* Bible studies with them.

But of all the women in the congregation he had sex with, his favorite was the preacher's wife. She was about thirty-five years old and was built for sex. She had no children and her body was tight from working out five times a week. Her large natural breasts begged to be sucked and her perfect ass begged to be fucked.

The first time they met, she invited him over for fried chicken. He had already been through this several times with some of the other women so he was already hard before they even started eating the chicken. He couldn't keep his eyes off her breasts. She was squeezed into a too-tight sundress and the big babies were about to pop out. He ached to get his hands on her. She, on the other hand, could see the thick bulge through his pants and couldn't wait to get her lips around that thing. But they couldn't just launch themselves at each other too quickly. After all, she had gone to a lot of trouble to cook the chicken. And besides, they were having homemade ice cream for dessert.

"So, I guess the Reverend isn't coming back for a while?" Red said as he bit into a chicken leg. He was already drooling at the prospect of licking the preacher's wife's pussy. The chicken was a poor substitute, even though it was extremely good.

"He's going to be gone all day. He's gone to check out some new hymnals," she said, crossed her legs and took a bite of fried okra.

Red finished his leg and cleared his throat.

"Could I have a breast please," he said and smiled. He looked directly at her breasts.

"Um...yeah. Anything you want. Just ask," she said and picked up the bowl of chicken and leaned over to him brushing her breasts against his face. He couldn't control himself and took a nibble through her dress as she leaned into him. She moaned a little and went back to her seat.

Red took a bite out of the chicken breast. "This is good."

The preacher's wife rubbed her pussy a little bit as she watched him eat.

"Uh huh."

After a couple more moments, she noticed that his glass was empty.

"Let me get you some more tea, Red."

"I would like that," he said and rubbed her ass a little as she walked past him to the refrigerator.

She brought the pitcher back to the table and poured a little tea, but couldn't help but splash a little on his lap.

"Oops," she said.

"That's ok," Red said. "It's only tea."

"Oh, no it's not ok. I'm gonna have to clean that up."

"Ok," Red said.

With that, the preacher's wife got down on her knees and began to lick up the tea from the front of his pants. Red's hard-on kicked into high gear. She unzipped his pants and before it even had a chance to stop bouncing, she started sucking him off. After a few strokes, she deepthroated him. All eleven inches. He was amazed. It was the first time anyone had ever deepthroated him completely. He knew that he was definitely staying for dessert.

After she sucked him almost to the point of ejaculation, she pulled up her dress and climbed up on the table. She spread her legs and pulled his face down to her pussy. She wasn't wearing any panties and she was so wet that she was dripping. Red loved eating pussy and he dove in with wild abandon, licking and sucking her clit. She pulled his head in close and hunched his face until she had an orgasm.

After that, she changed position and leaned over the table.

"Fuck me doggie style, church boy. I want to see how deep that big dick of yours can go."

Red stuck it in so fast that it took her breath away. He immediately started pounding her with everything he had. The dishes shook on the table and at one point, the chicken was in danger of falling into the floor. The preacher's wife had the good fortune to grab it before it did though.

"Fuck me harder!" She ordered him.

He complied, pumping her with everything he had.

She came four twice before he breathlessly told her that he was about to cum.

"I want you to shoot it in my mouth," she said and pulled him out of her and got down on her knees and began to deepthroat him until he shot his whole load down her throat. After he finished, she swallowed and took a sip of tea.

"Now, let's get back to our chicken."

Over the course of the rest of the meal, Red learned that the preacher was impotent and didn't mind for her to go around screwing other men. Just so long as they weren't in the congregation. That was one of his biggest rules. No one from the congregation.

Just after they finished their ice cream, to their chagrin, the preacher walked in, carrying a box of new hymnals. He took one look at them, sitting there in the nude and the hymnals dropped to the floor.

"Damn it! June! I told you not to fuck anybody from the church!"

"It's ok, Grover. He's a good boy and he's got a big...heart. He won't say nothing." She looked at Red. "Will you, Red?"

Red thought about it for a minute. This was the chance he had been waiting for.

"I won't say anything on one condition."

Both the preacher and the preacher's wife looked at each other and then looked at him with a great amount of consternation.

"How much do you want?" The preacher sighed.

Red smiled. "I don't want any money. I just want you to let me start preaching."

At that the preacher and his wife looked at each other with a look of befuddlement. Suddenly, the preacher started smiling.

"That's the best blackmail I've ever paid, boy. You've got yourself a deal."

The preacher's wife reached over and rubbed Red's penis.

"He loves it when he gets to mentor another preacher."

And so he got started. His relationship with the preacher and his wife got even closer, with him coming over several times a week to service her and for the preacher to give him tips on how to deliver effective sermons.

After graduating from high school, he started preaching wherever he could. His sermons were typical fire and brimstone but soon, due to his young age and enthusiasm, he developed quite a following, especially among the homeless and downtrodden. These were people who always touched his heart, especially because they were so easy to manipulate. He soon figured out that if he gave them food and clothing, they would do pretty much anything he wanted.

The girls were no exception. One of his favorite things was to take a scruffy young woman, clean her up and take her back to his place for a *laying on of hands*. He would cure her of her ailments and give her a job. Then she would become a part of his inner circle for a while and provide him with the services he couldn't receive from any of his male co-workers. This would go on until he found another girl to help. He didn't want to deny any of them.

Because of his predilection for the homeless, he called his church the *Cardboard Cathedral*. However, he referred to his ministry as a whole as *The Church of What's Happenin' Now* to stress the immediacy of his message. He wanted everyone to know that his church was not about the past, and not about what people had done in their past, but rather what they were doing now and what they were going to do in the future. It was a message of forgiveness and inclusion.

He ran thrift stores and missions. He gave the homeless jobs. He gave them food and clothing and they gave him loyalty. Rapidly he expanded his empire. Eventually, he was able to buy a small TV station and from that he was able to realize his dream of starting his own cable network. He had everything a man could want. He advised several heads of state on spiritual matters and he could get any woman he wanted. But now he was finding himself getting bored. He really felt as though he had done all there was to do as far as being a TV preacher went. He was jaded and blasé. Sitting there in the recliner with the girl's mouth on his dick made it all too clear to him.

"That's good, baby," he said as he shot his load into the girl's mouth.

She licked her lips and cleaned him off.

"Do you want me to do anything else, Brother Red?" She said sweetly.

"No, that's ok, Sister Gwen. Just go back and make sure that there's plenty of mattresses in the mission."

She smiled and left the room.

Naturally, Red's dalliance with the ladies of the church had shaped his attitudes about sex. Unlike a lot of the other religious people he knew, he didn't have any hang-ups and misconceptions about sex. To him it was a great thing. It was about having fun and giving others pleasure.

Some people would have thought that his viewpoints on sex were a little too open for a man of the cloth and he would have to say that he didn't blame them. Not everyone saw sex the way he did. In fact, he saw sex between consenting adults as completely natural and healthy. It was no moral gray area in his book. The trouble was, he couldn't come out and say this to anyone. He hated this. He felt dishonest about keeping his attitudes towards sex secret. However, he knew that if he came out and started preaching free love and whatnot that he would be completely alienated from his congregation and he could possibly lose his church. But on the other hand, he realized that he would probably also help a lot of people by letting them know that they weren't reprobates and perverts because they enjoyed a good threesome every now and again. He was constantly at battle with himself over this. However, he always took the path of least resistance and kept it secret. He figured that the good he did by keeping his mainstream congregation far outweighed what he would achieve if he came out and said that fucking was okay.

Red flicked on the TV and DVD player. He pressed play. He had been watching and re-watching the same porno movie for the last month or so. It was a nasty little film called *Black Bra and Panties* and starred a girl named Josie Bistro. In it, she went around trying to figure out where she had lost her expensive black bra and panties. Since she was quite an active girl, she was having a real problem tracking her belongings down. Also, she kept getting sidetracked by all the sex she kept getting involved in. He was so intrigued that he just couldn't stop watching it.

Actually, there was a little more to it than that, he thought that the girl was his destiny. Long ago, when he had first started out in the ministry he had started having a recurring dream about being married. Aside from the church, he never experienced such happiness as he did in his dream. It was always the same. He was at a party and was looking everywhere for his wife. He wasn't panicked, but excited about finding her. He searched all over the house until finally he heard her. She was out in the backyard. He walked outside and saw her. She was down on all fours and surrounded by naked men. She was sucking everything that was presented to her and getting fucked by everyone. She was half-wearing a black bra and her black panties were hanging on the heel of her pump. He was so happy in this dream. His wife was beautiful, red-haired and was an absolute slut. When he had first seen *Black Bra and Panties*, he had almost fainted. The girl of his dreams was Josie.

It was fate. But how could he ever meet her? He was a famous televangelist and she was a porno actress. How could you make something like that work?

As he watched her take it from a couple of meatheads, a light went off in his head.

He snapped his fingers and picked up the phone.

3

"**G**et it, Girl! Get it!"

Josie sucked the big black cock with even more abandon. The urging of the director wasn't even a factor in her performance. Between the cock in her mouth and the one dogging her from behind, she could barely pay attention to a word he was saying. After all, it wasn't every day that she was sucking the cock of Cedric Gunn and getting fucked silly by Jerome Crank. These two were legends in the industry. They were favorites of most of the porn girls due to their size and skill and here she was doing both of them at the same time!

Josie had dutifully reported to the set the day after she had gotten back in town. It was a rented house in a quiet, upscale residential area. Most of the neighbors were completely unaware that a porno movie was being shot there. While there were a few cars parked in the driveway, it looked more like the house was being shown to prospective buyers rather than a den of iniquity. The only giveaway was the abundance of large breasted, scantily clad women cavorting around.

She took a glance around her as she deepthroated the thick nine-incher. Other porno girls and guys lounged around reading magazines and talking to the crew and each other. Some were nude and some weren't. She was glad to be working. She sympathized with the actors because she always got bored when she waited around for her scenes to begin. At least it was her turn to work. But even more than that, she was glad to be fucking.

The nubian behind her pounded her like she had never been pounded before. He was by far the most aggressive partner she had ever had. He was literally pumping the orgasms out of her. She had at least three without even trying. One of him would have been enough for any girl, along with the massive penis in front of her, she thought she had died and gone to big cock heaven.

The director could barely contain himself as he jumped around giving them instructions.

"Now switch! I want to see that one there fuck her."

The two studs switched around and Josie was eager to get filled up with dick again. This time she lay on her back and got it missionary style while she leaned over and slurped on the big black cock.

"Suck it, girl," Jerome moaned as she licked the head of his dick. She could taste herself on him and she began to look longingly over at the naked girls sitting around awaiting their scenes. This made her suck even harder.

If she had thought the other guy fucked hard, he was nothing compared to this one. He was like a wild man. While the other guy pumped the orgasms out of her, this one was literally jarring them loose.

"Don't stop! Don't stop!" She said as she came for the third time that scene.

The stud fucking her just grinned and picked up the pace.

Eventually, the director signaled for the guys to cum and both disengaged themselves from her and masturbated themselves into her mouth. She eagerly lapped up the cum and cleaned their penises off. When the cameraman got in close to get a good shot of the cum on her face, she couldn't resist winking at the camera.

"You missed some," Cedric said and pointed to his dick. She smiled at the camera and licked up what she had missed.

The director was absolutely beaming after the scene.

"I think I'm gonna have go to jerk off now," he said and slapped the guys on the back. He winked at Josie and she playfully went after his crotch. She wasn't serious though because he was happily married to a woman who knew absolutely nothing about what he did for a living. Most of the other girls also tried to stay clear of him because they didn't want all the hassle that would ensue if his wife ever found out about him, but still, he had a way of working his charm with some of the younger girls. Josie couldn't help but roll her eyes as a fairly new young starlet followed him into the bathroom. She went to another part of the house and took a shower.

After she finished cleaning herself up, she put on a tight t-shirt and cutoff jeans and went to the kitchen. The two black guys were already in there eating some catered lasagna.

"Girl, you were absolutely fan-fucking-tastic," Cedric said as he chewed his lasagna.

"Well, let me tell you, when a girl gets fucked like that, she doesn't have a choice but to be fan-fucking-tastic," Josie laughed.

Jerome and Cedric laughed.

"You two finished for the day?" Josie asked.

At that, a pretty Latina walked up.

"This one had better not be finished, we've still got a scene," she said grabbing onto Jerome's dick though his pants. Jerome was instantly hard. She then playfully punched Josie on the arm. "I hope you didn't use up all his juice."

Josie playfully punched her back.

"Carmen, from the looks of him, I think there's plenty left to go around."

Jerome's pants now looked like a tent trying to open. He cracked up laughing.

"What about you, Josie? You got any more scenes?" He asked.

"I think me and miss thing here has one later." She winked at Carmen who leaned in and began to feel her up starting at her tits.

"You girls, keep that shit up, I'm gonna have to let this dog out!" Jerome said and pointed to his about-to-burst pants.

"Me too," Cedric said.

Carmen and Josie collapsed into giggles. Cedric and Jerome were probably the funniest two guys in porn. If they hadn't been so well-endowed, they could've probably become comedians, Josie thought. Not to say that comedians weren't well-endowed, but most of the ones that Josie had screwed had been hung like buttons.

"I don't think I'm gonna be able to wait for my scene. I'm gonna have to have me a taste right now," Carmen said and got down on her knees and extricated Jerome's cock from his pants.

While Carmen sucked, Josie grabbed a paper plate and started to serve herself some lasagna when all of sudden the director came running into the kitchen.

"Get your clothes on! Someone's outside!"

"Is it a cop?" Jerome said and continued to eat his lasagna.

"I don't know!" The director whined. "I can't go to jail. My wife will kill me!"

"You have a permit, don't you?" Carmen asked nonchalantly as she reluctantly let go of Jerome's dick.

"A permit! I didn't know I had to have a permit." Suddenly he grabbed Josie. "Here, you look innocent. Go answer the door."

Josie looked at him in shock. She didn't relish the thought of going to jail either. She didn't think shooting a porno was illegal, but she didn't want to find out the hard way that it wasn't.

"What about her?" Josie said and pointed to Carmen.

"No, she looks like a slut. It's got to be you. You look like somebody's daughter."

Jerome and Cedric winced at the comment and Carmen looked like she was ready to punch him.

"Shouldn't we go out the back?" Josie asked.

"No!" He shrieked. "If it's the cops, they'll be back there. Just go answer the door and tell them that we're having…"

"An Amway party?" Cedric suggested.

"Yes, an Amway party! Tell them we're having an Amway party!"

"What if I don't want to?" Josie countered.

"Do you want to work in the business again?"

"Man, that shit's cold," Cedric said under his breath.

"I'm serious. Do it or you're blacklisted." The director was almost foaming at the mouth at this point. His eyes were bugged out and he looked on the verge of losing it. "You won't fuck on film again."

"Oh, ok, then, I'll do it."

Reluctantly, Josie went to the front door. She noticed that the other actors had hastily dressed themselves and were sitting around with the crew like they were in church or something.

She opened the door, fully expecting to see a cop. She was a little surprised at what she saw.

It was an old slick haired guy and a sexy young woman and they were both carrying Bibles. While appearing to be clean, the old guy had the stench of poverty and homelessness. He was weatherbeaten from spending too much time outside and his suit was cheap, like it had been donated by somebody. The girl on the other hand, looked like a model or something and was dressed in a smart navy blue business suit. They were definitely the odd couple.

"Can I help you?" Josie asked.

The old man smiled.

"Sister, if you have a minute, I can tell you something that will change your life."

4

Getting ready for a swing party was always a big event at Josie's parent's house.

Yes, there was at least one thing about her parents that Josie didn't know.

"Do I look ridiculous, honey?" Hal asked as he put on an enormous purple fur hat.

"You look great, dear," Priscilla answered as she sat on the bed fastening the strap on her six inch heel.

"I mean I really look like a pimp, don't I?" Hal said as he continued to survey himself in the bedroom mirror. The Pimps and Hookers Ball was only a once a year thing at their swing club and it was absolutely imperative for Hal to look his best. He was trying to maximize his potential and seize the moment and accomplish every other self-actualizing objective that he talked about in his seminars. Hal Bistro was definitely a man who practiced what he preached. However, he couldn't actually tell Priscilla that this was what he was doing because she hated for him to talk about his job. It bored her to tears.

"Well, I would definitely be your ho," Priscilla purred as she sidled up to Hal and started to stroke his penis through his pants.

"You're gonna have to slow down, baby. You don't want to waste it all on me. You can have me any time."

"I think I've got plenty to go around," she said and got down on her knees and took his penis out of his pink velvet pants.

"Well, I don't know if I do...oooh yeah, baby. Suck it just right that." He placed his hands on the back of her head and rubbed it as she deepthroated him. Up and down, up and down, he knew that she was going for it, so he might as well go along for the ride.

Priscilla pushed her short skirt up and began to rub her pussy. Hal could see that it was already wet. It was dripping and glistening and the sight of it made him that much harder. Occasionally she licked the hand she was rubbing her pussy with and sometimes she pushed it into Hal's mouth. After a few minutes, he heard her breathing quicken a little and she started to suck just a little harder. She was going to cum. A couple of seconds later, he could feel her body shudder and he was unable to hold it in any longer. He began to squirt his cum deep down into her throat. She looked him square in the eyes and gulped it like she was drinking a milkshake. Not one drop was wasted. She took the whole load. There would be no mess to clean up tonight. Not that there ever was.

Hal chuckled and gave her a kiss as she got to her feet. "Not bad for a couple of forty-year olds."

Priscilla lit a cigarette. "God, if I was as horny when I was in my twenties as I am now, I think I would have stayed pregnant."

The two of them finished dressing and went downstairs. Hal definitely looked the part in his purple hat and pink velvet suit. He had bought the outfit six months earlier at a yard sale. He had been chomping at the bit for this night. Priscilla would look hot wearing a burlap sack, but in her slutty, tight black dress and classic pumps, she looked good enough to eat.

After they got downstairs, Hal looked at his watch. "Well, it looks like we made it with time to spare."

"Wow, we've got a whole ten minutes. Do you want me to fix you a drink before Bob and Jenny show up?" Bob and Jenny were an over-tanned, oily but good looking couple around the same age as Hal and Priscilla. The two couples swung fairly regularly and considered each other to be good friends. They also played golf together occasionally.

"Only if you're fixing yourself one."

"Well, I am. I want to get a little bit loosened up for this thing. You know I've been a little distracted what with Josie not being here and all."

"I know, dear. You just like to worry."

"I know. I just don't like her being all the way out there in California by herself."

She walked over to the bar and began to fix two martinis. "Don't think it's about time that we told her about us?" She said as she took the vodka from the freezer. "After all, she is a porno actress. I think she'll be able to handle it."

Hal shook his head. "We've been over this before, Pris. I just don't think it's a good idea. You know part of the reason that she's in porn is to rebel against us. Can you imagine what it would do to her if she found out that we're probably more sexually active than she is? It would really upset her world."

"You're probably right," Priscilla said as she poured the vermouth. "She might think she's got to go to even greater extremes to shock us. She might start using drugs."

"Or she might become a religious fanatic," Hal said.

"I don't know what I would do if that happened. I shudder to think of it."

"Well, maybe it wouldn't be so bad."

"Then again, maybe it would," she said.

Priscilla brought the drinks over and they began to sip. Hal lit a cigarette.

"You know, I can't help but be a little jealous of her. She's really got her priorities straight at such a young age."

Hal took a big sip. "Yeah, she's got her priorities straight, but I just wish she would be a little more concerned about her future. She can have just as much sex being a banker or a lawyer as she can being a porno actress."

"She's young. She just doesn't realize it."

Just then, the doorbell rang.

"They're here." Priscilla quickly downed her drink and went over and opened the door.

"Hey, swingers!" Bob said, swinging a big black walking stick and sporting a lavender polyester leisure suit. His platform shoes made him a full five inches taller than Jenny who was dressed in a tight red tube dress and go-go boots with six-inch heels. Bob looked like a pimp, sure enough, but he was definitely not pimp enough to out-pimp Hal.

"What up, pimp!" Hal said as he finished his drink. "Do you two want one?"

"No, we're fine," Jenny said.

"I had my drink before you two came over," Priscilla said and winked.

They all started laughing and walked to the minivan. Hal and Priscilla couldn't wait to see who was going to be at the party. They weren't going to worry any more about telling Josie their dirty little secret. It could wait until later. They had plenty of time.

5

Josie parked her Nissan on the sun drenched, tree lined street and walked the short distance to Gunter Bumsen's house. A guy washing his car dropped the hose when he saw her in her lowcut jeans and halter top. She was definitely smoking today. However, sex was not on her mind. She was here to see Gunter. Gunter was a German porn actor with whom Josie had had the pleasure to work on several occasions. Over in Europe, he was almost mainstream. He was always being asked to appear at openings of sex shops, book stores and shopping malls. Over here, he was just another porno actor. He was typically full of bullshit, saying that he split his time between the states and Europe because he just couldn't stand the celebrity at times. Of course, he also complained that people in the states didn't have enough of an appreciation for him. His ego wouldn't let him see that while he was a muscular, somewhat good looking guy, he was still just a porno actor. His euro-mullet didn't help his cause much either.

While Josie had always enjoyed working with him because he had a large penis and really knew how to fuck, she wasn't here today to discuss business. She was here to talk about the metaphysical. He was a self-styled mystical type and, for some reason, when it came to spiritual matters, all the porno types always looked to him for advice. Apparently none of them had ever caught on to the fact that he didn't know anything.

After the appearance of the weird old guy and gorgeous girl at the porno shoot, Josie had been thrown for a loop. She had taken the old guy up on his assertion that he could change her life and had allowed him into the house. Of course, the director immediately threw them out so they had to talk in the driveway.

At first, Josie had begun to feel a little guilty about doing porno when she was confronted with the idea of talking to a religious person. But the old man shook his head at such thoughts. He also couldn't help but drool at the sight of Josie in her tight t-shirt and cutoff jeans.

"What would you say if I told you it doesn't matter what you do or what you've done. What would you say if I told you that you are accepted, no matter what."

"Unless you've killed somebody, of course," the pretty girl, who had introduced herself as Sister Gwen, added. "You haven't killed anybody, have you?"

"Um…no. I still don't understand what you've talking about," Josie said.

The old man, whose name was Brother Farlin, lit up a cigarette. "We're talking about Brother Red Hair and his Cardboard Cathedral. You know, *The Church of*

What's Happenin' Now. We want you and your friends to come down and sit in on a service. We want you to come on down and see what we're all about."

"But why? We're just porno people. I would've thought that someone like Brother Red Hair would hate us."

The pretty girl started smiling and shook her head.

"Oh, no. Brother Red may preach fire and brimstone, but he doesn't have anything against people who work in the sex industry. He thinks it's a shame that you're so ostracized when you have so much to offer."

Josie couldn't help but notice that the girl was checking her out.

"Heck, I used to be a prostitute before I started to going to the Cardboard Cathedral."

"And he didn't care?" Josie asked incredulously.

"Heck no. He said come on in. We need some more whores!" Sister Gwen laughed.

Brother Farlin nodded his head, not once taking his eyes off Josie's breasts.

"Well, I'll think about going some time then," Josie said to get them to move along.

Sister Gwen and Brother Farlin beamed at each other.

"One thing though," the girl said. "All new girls have to wear black bras and panties. It's very symbolic to Brother Hair. He insists on it."

"That's kind of odd, but I guess if it's symbolic..." Josie said. She paused for a second. "You know? I did a movie about black underwear once."

"Really?" Sister Gwen said and uncomfortably cleared her throat. She then pulled her shirt down to show Josie her black bra. She smiled. "I always wear mine."

After shaking hands and telling her how much they looked forward to seeing her in church, the two then handed Josie some pamphlets and tract literature and walked off. Josie went back into the house and did her scene.

Usually, this sort of thing didn't affect her. The whole religion thing. However, for some reason, she just couldn't get her mind around it. She had read and re-read the tracts which were mostly concerned with how everyone was going to hell. They also stressed the importance of tithing and how you should help your fellow man.

No, it wasn't the tracts. It also wasn't the fact that she kept seeing Brother Red Hair on the TV every time she turned it on.

It was the comment about the black bra and panties. That was what had her puzzled. What the hell did that mean? When she had told Marcy about it, she had suggested that she go see Gunter.

"If anybody will know, he will," Marcy said.

So, that's what she was doing.

"Hallo, Baby," Gunter said as he opened the door.

"Hello, Gunter," she said and kissed him on his cheeks in the European fashion to which he was accustomed. She also overlooked the annoying fact that he referred to everyone, male and female alike as "baby." For some reason, when he had learned English, he had gotten the idea that this was a cool thing to do and no one had ever had the heart to tell him differently.

They went into the living room and sat down. A couple of girls were sitting on the floor with their legs crossed meditating. Josie pointed to them as if to ask if they would be disturbing them.

"Oh, no, baby. They are so high, they still they think they are in Belgium!" He laughed.

They had a seat on a large beanbag sofa. On the coffee table in front of them sat a very new deck of Tarot cards. These were strictly for show, because Gunter had no clue as how to read them. If asked to give a reading, he would always say something to the effect that he had a spiritual blockage and would be unable to do it accurately. He would defer to his magic eight ball instead.

"So, baby, what can I help you with?"

Josie explained what was going on. Gunter nodded and gestured in a way that suggested that he understood exactly what she was talking about.

"Marcy said that if anybody would know, you would."

Gunter pondered for a moment, visibly turning it over in his mind.

"While I have devoted my life to studying the great mysteries, I have to admit that this is quite unusual."

"Yes?"

"Let me pause to think for a moment, baby. I have to try to channel the power of the ancients to discover the answer to the riddle that you seek."

At that he closed his eyes and started chanting. To Josie, he sounded like he was reading off the periodic chart or something. She didn't say anything, though. He was supposed to be "at one" with things.

After a few minutes, he suddenly smiled and opened his eyes. "I think I have your answer. I was able to channel the spirit of an ancient medicine man. He gave me the answer you seek."

Josie's eyes opened wide.

"What is it? What does it mean?" She asked excitedly.

Gunter smiled even more widely.

"The medicine man thinks that maybe this preacher just likes black bras and panties, baby."

Josie looked at him incredulously. Was that it? Was that the opinion of a man who was supposedly spiritually in tune?

Gunter leaned back and smiled.

"So, baby, now that I've answered your question, do you want to screw now?"

Josie hadn't really thought about it, but she was feeling a little horny.

"Sure, why not?" She said and took off her skirt.

Gunter was hard instantly and Josie was down on her knees worshipping his cock within seconds. The two stoned girls just looked on with a vague detachment. It was like they were watching television or something.

Josie went to work on his cock like a pro. He was muttering in German and the pre-cum came up fast. Josie fingered herself as she blew him, occasionally tasting herself.

Her head bobbed up and down like a machine as she brought up his cum.

"You better slow down, baby. I'm not going to get to fuck you if you keep that up," Gunter said, slowing her head down.

"Well, let's just get down to the fucking then," Josie said matter of factly and crawled up into his lap, putting his dick in her pussy with one fluid movement.

"Let's do it this way," Josie said as she started to grind against him.

Gunter's eyes rolled to the back of his head as she flexed her vaginal muscles around his big dick. She rode him like a mechanical bull, except she was in no danger of getting thrown.

"Ugh, I love your big cock," Josie moaned and quickened her pace. She sped up to the point where their skin was making slapping noises as they went together. She groaned as she crescendoed into a massive orgasm. Gunter struggled to hold on and was relieved when she finally came.

"Where do you want it, baby?" Gunter said breathlessly.

"Cum in my pussy," she said.

At that, Gunter squirted a massive load deep inside of her. She started shuddering again as he pumped her full. She was having another orgasm.

After they were finished, Josie put her clothes on and resolved that she had to start going to church.

6

"**B**rothers and sisters! Are you ready! Are you down with What's Happenin' Now? Are you up with what's happenin' today?" A big black guy in an expensive light blue suit smiled broadly as he stood on the stage of the Cardboard Cathedral. The congregation exploded into amens and hallelujahs.

At that the big Hammond organ at the back of the stage started playing the most rocked out and boogie woogied up gospel music that Josie had ever heard. The drums joined in and the big black guy started clapping his hands. The congregation followed suit. "Amen, brothers and sisters!"

The guy at the organ, the slick haired guy who Josie had seen being tied up and thrown off the stage on television, was going crazy playing the organ. He was like some sort of Pentecostal Liberace or something.

"And here he is, brothers and sisters, Brother Red Hair!" The big black guy stepped to the side as Brother Red Hair walked very fast out to the stage. He was all smiles and was already sweating. He wore an expensive tan suit and a very stylish scarlet tie.

"Thank you, Brother Abernathy," Red said to the big black guy.

"Hallalujah!"

"Hallalujah!" Red answered back.

The organ music died down and the church grew quiet.

"Brother Myrtlewood is revved up on that organ, ain't he bruthas and sistas?"

Brother Myrtlewood Green beamed at the recognition by Red.

Red surveyed the congregation and was extremely proud of what he was seeing. He was amazed every time he preached to such a big crowd. There was so much love out there that it overwhelmed him. He was determined that this was going to be one his best sermons ever. He knew that his very special lady was out there somewhere and he had to make it count. He was so psyched he could barely stand still.

After Red began his sermon, he began to run around the stage like a madman. He preached and hollered, always eliciting a chorus of "Amen, Brother!" or other sayings like that. Occasionally people would simply raise their hands up and wave them in the air.

Josie sat up in the farthest reaches of the building, spellbound by what she was seeing. She had never seen a religious sermon like this. She had grown up an Episcopalian and was not used to people moving around during the service.

"Baby, is it making you horny?"

Gunter sat beside her. He had agreed to come along only after Josie had promised to be in one of his movies. Besides, he was sort of intrigued by the phenomenon of Brother Red Hair. Being a European, this was even more far out for him than it was for Josie. Marcy sat on her other side. He also noticed the bevy of beauties who were scattered throughout the church. They all wore headsets and he figured that they were probably part of Red's organization. The sight of these girls was not lost on Marcy and Josie either.

"Shut up, I'm trying to listen," he said after Marcy winked at him.

They were both wearing dresses. Gunter, however, looked more like he was going to a nightclub than he was a church. He had on a pair of black leather pants and a half open silk shirt.

Josie looked around her at the other members of the congregation. It contained people from all walks of life. There were homeless people and streetwalkers as well as people in nice clothes. There were old people, young people, thin people and fat people. You name it, they were there. Josie also took a look around the Cardboard Cathedral. It wasn't really made of cardboard, as she had sort of suspected. It was just the old civic coliseum. It was decorated with purple curtains and a scant few other decorations. Mostly, it was just your typical auditorium. Still, it was filled with something that was absolutely indescribable. It was filled with the force of Red's personality, but more than that, it was filled with love. The place was huge and it was absolutely packed.

She was just able to see Sister Gwen and Brother Farlin sitting down on the front row.

As Josie listened to Red's words, she couldn't help but feel something stirring in deep inside her. Her hormones were surging at the sight of Brother Red down there shouting out the message. She just didn't know what was coming over her. Maybe it was the heat. The coliseum was pretty hot and stuffy. Maybe it was the pantyhose. She certainly wasn't used to wearing anything like that. She wasn't even sure why she had worn them. She guessed it was because her mother had always told her to wear pantyhose whenever she went to church. "It's more ladylike," she had said.

Of course, she remembered to wear her black bra and panties. Perhaps that's why she was so constricted. Was a person supposed to wear panties with pantyhose? Since she never wore underwear, it was a little unclear for her. Then again, maybe the cause was something else. It was more like animal magnetism. She could certainly tell that Brother Red had a lot of that.

"How about now, baby?" Gunter said again. "I know I'm horny."

Marcy crossed and uncrossed her legs and smiled at him. She looked over at Josie who was entranced.

The thing about it was that Josie really was horny. She was really feeling to feel lightheaded. Her breathing was shallow and she felt an odd sort of excitement from the service. She ached to start playing with herself, but didn't because she was in church.

Of course, Brother Red Hair knew for a fact that she was in the audience. It was more than just a gut feeling. His staff had been on the lookout for her. He had to struggle not to get a hard-on when he finally spotted her. He fought the urge to masturbate in front of the congregation. Still, he had to get closer to her. When he saw her, began to play to her. As he did this, he suddenly had an idea.

He stopped preaching for a second and took out his handkerchief and mopped his brow.

"Brothers and Sisters," he began. "I'm really feeling the spirit today. I'm really feeling it take a hold of me. Does that ever happen to you? The spirit just gets a hold of you and makes you just want to run."

He looked feverishly around the congregation and was pleased to see that Josie was transfixed by his service.

Red gave a big smile and suddenly took off running the aisles of the church.

"Whoooo!" He yelled and waved his hands above his hands as he ran.

He ran down one and then the next until finally he was running down the one in which Josie was seated.

Josie's heartbeat quickened as he approached. Her breathing quickened and she could feel herself becoming flushed. Even Gunter and Marcy stopped their flirting as he approached. Her mouth began to water at the sight of his enormous penis which was bouncing within his pants at every step. Her head swam more and more with each approaching step. She was being consumed with horniness and it felt as all the blood was running out of her head. It was just too much to take as she gazed up upon Red's smiling face, growing closer and closer. His cock…

Then suddenly, he was beside Josie.

She looked up at him in awe and when he smiled and put his hand out and touched her on the head, her world suddenly went black.

7

"**B**rothers and sisters, puhleeze give the young lady some air! Puhleeze, step back and give me some room to work!" Red waved off the crowd as they gathered around Josie's prone body. She had been unconscious for about thirty seconds and Red knew that he was going to have to do something quick.

"Please step back, brothers and sisters, Brother Red is gonna heal this young lady," Brother Abernathy said as he stepped up and started working as crowd control. Brother Myrtlewood picked up the pace on the organ and soon people were running the aisles and rejoicing in time to the music. They clapped their hands like crazy people and if it had been a rock concert instead of a church service, there would have surely been stage diving. Some people even began hopping over the pews. It was an amazing sight. To an outside observer, it would have looked more like an insane asylum than a church.

Marcy was down at Josie's side, fanning her with her hand, trying to get her to wake up.

"Josie, wake up!" She tried to shoo people away. "Please give her some air!"

She turned to Gunter. "Pick her up and let's take her to the hospital!"

Gunter stepped over Josie and bent down to pick her up, but Brother Abernathy gently pushed him aside.

"It'll be okay. Let Brother Red here take a look."

"You're kidding, right?" Gunter sputtered.

Red smiled and knelt over Josie. "No, Brother, he's not kidding. I'm gonna heal this here girl!"

Brother Abernathy looked knowingly at Marcy and Gunter. "He's gonna lay his hands on her."

Red grinned up at them like he was Buddha or something. Being the charismatic individual he was, he had been through this dozens of times. Pretty girls all over the world had swooned over him. Sometimes, they would just get so worked up that they would just faint right there on the spot. This was nothing new and he knew just the trick to get her to come to.

Red knelt down over her and placed his hands on her stomach. He gently rubbed it and worked his way up to her breasts. He rubbed them slowly, cupping them and really giving them a sensual massage. He noticed with glee that Josie was wearing the black bra. He was certain that she had worn the panties as well. This was almost too much to take. He looked over at Marcy and wondered if she had remembered as well. He gave Marcy a little wink.

Marcy gave a slight smile back and noticed with mixed feelings the enormous bulge growing in Red's trousers.

"What do you think you're doing?" Marcy said, not taking her eyes off the bulge. Was it ever going to stop getting larger, she thought to herself.

"Oh, nobody lays on hands like Brother Red," a toothless old woman exclaimed and went back to dancing and waving her hands in the air and speaking in tongues.

Brother Abernathy also gave her a little smile. She noticed that he had an erection as well. It was nothing to sneeze at either.

Red continued to work on Josie, rubbing her breasts and putting one hand up her skirt. He rubbed her pussy a little harder than he had her breasts, and suddenly she started moving a little bit. She was still unconscious but she was waking up.

Red moved his body so his erection was right in front of her face, and started to really work her pussy. After a few seconds, the still unconscious Julie began to make a sucking motion with her lips. Red moved his penis, which was still in his pants, to her mouth and she began to gently gnaw on it. He suddenly picked up the pace on her pussy and after a few more seconds, she began to buck and soon was flailing and gasping with a gigantic orgasm.

Then, as she came, she came to, still mouthing Red's penis.

Everybody in the congregation began to cheer.

She looked up at Red, who was smiling benevolently down at her. He removed the finger he had had inside her and licked it. Then he smoothed her hair.

Some women would have felt violated after being molested in their sleep like that, but Josie amazingly was not. She looked up at Red and felt a devotion that she had never felt for anyone before in her life. It was like a message had been sent to her and for the first time in her life she truly felt like she had a purpose. She knew what she was meant to do. She knew that she was meant to follow this man.

Brother Abernathy reached down and helped her up, being sure to feel her up a little as he steadied her on her feet. "You were out for quite a few minutes, Miss. But thankfully, Brother Red here was able to bring you back."

People patted Red on the back.

"It wasn't me, brothers and sisters. I'm just a tool. I think we know who was responsible." Red tried not to sound too insincere. He wasn't really, but sometimes playing the part of the TV preacher was even a little bit more than even he could bear.

Gunter and Marcy were flabbergasted. Marcy couldn't believe that Red's penis was so large and Gunter couldn't believe what he had just seen Red get away with. Maybe he was in the wrong game, after all. Being in porn meant that you could get laid any time you wanted, but the money wasn't always that great. But from what he could tell about being a preacher, it was about getting laid and making lots of money. His mind was swimming with possibilities.

Josie stared around for a minute at the crowd that had gathered around her. Brother Myrtlewood was wailing on the Hammond and people were dancing in the aisles in joyous celebration of Brother Red's laying on of hands.

She looked at Red who continued to smile at her. "When is your next service? I want to be here."

Marcy looked at his erection. It hadn't shrunk one bit. It strained to be released from his pants and she couldn't help but moisten her lips at the sight of it. Still, she didn't really know about all of this. She had been raised a strict Seventh Day Adventist and had had enough of church when she was a kid. She sure didn't want to get that started again. But then she happened to catch a glimpse of Brother Abernathy. His penis was still hard as well and she could catch the outline of the head through his tight thin pants. She felt her face flush and her pussy get warm. The sight of the two monster cocks was more than enough to convince her.

"Me, too," she said without hesitating.

Gunter looked around at all the gorgeous girls that Red had working for him and realized that there might be something to this religion thing after all. He might learn how to start his own thing.

"I want to join as well."

Red put his arms around them and gave them a big hug.

"Welcome home, brother and sisters. Welcome home."

8

"**D**o you think that this dildo is big enough?" Priscilla said as she picked up a black nine-inch jelly dong. She liked the feel of it, but she didn't want to buy just any old thing. She had done that many times in the past and, as a result, had lots of sextoys that she rarely used. Of course, they were always a hit at the swing parties she and Hal hosted, but this time she really wanted something that was going to knock her socks off.

"I don't know, honey. You know how hot you get sometimes," Hal said as he inspected a Swedish cock ring set. He wasn't really that much into cock rings, but what the hell, you only live once, he thought. He also wondered if they were any different from the Dutch cock ring set he had gotten the previous year.

Priscilla and Hal were doing some shopping for Bob and Jenny's anniversary party. They had already bought presents for both Bob and Jenny and were now looking for something for themselves. Priscilla had bought Jenny an elaborate strap-on set and for Bob they had gotten a g-string with an elephant's head as the crotch piece. Naturally, this was a practical joke. They had also bought them a shiatsu massager. Priscilla couldn't wait to try out the strap-on on Jenny and Hal couldn't wait to watch.

"Do you have anything bigger than this?" Priscilla asked the clerk. He was a typically dumpy guy in his twenties with a shaved head and numerous facial piercings.

"The twelve-inchers are on the wall to your left," he said cheerfully.

"Oh, thanks."

As they looked at the brightly colored dildos, Priscilla turned to Hal.

"Do you think we should buy Josie something? After all, she's in the adult biz. She might really appreciate it."

Hal shook his head. "No, I don't think it's a good idea. She might think we're weird or something. You know how these kids are. It's okay if it's their idea, but if Mom and Dad come on board, all of a sudden, it's square."

"Oh, I understand what you're saying, but eventually, we'll have to tell her about us."

Hal sighed. "I know. But let's wait until the right time, okay?"

Priscilla nodded. "Whenever that is," she said under her breath.

Hal heard her, but didn't say anything.

"Oh, here's a nice one," she said and picked up a twelve inch black one.

"That is a good one. It'll fit into your strap-on thing, too."

"Yeah, you're right," she said.

After paying for their purchases, they went home.

"I'm gonna call her, just to see how's she doing," Hal said putting the bags down on the kitchen table. "She may try to call tonight while we're gone."

"Okay. I need to talk to her about what she wants me to do about her car tags, anyway," Priscilla said.

Hal picked up the phone.

"What time is it out there, Hal?"

Hal looked at his watch. "It's around two."

He dialed the number and Josie picked up after one ring.

"Oh, hello, baby. How's it going?" Hal asked.

Priscilla watched with a little interest as Hal listened to what sounded like an enormous amount of chattering coming from the other side of the line. This went on for a few minutes, with Hal interjecting a, "That's nice," or "Good for you," every so often. Eventually, Hal said goodbye absently and hung up the phone.

"Hal! Why did you hang up for? You knew I wanted to talk to her."

"Oh, I'm sorry," he mumbled and stared off into space.

"What's wrong? What did she say?"

Dazed, he looked at her, barely able to speak.

"She's not pregnant is she? Please don't say she's pregnant!" Priscilla was almost frantic.

Hal slowly shook his head.

"No, it's nothing like that. It's worse in a way. I guess you were right. We really should have told her about us. Maybe this wouldn't have happened. She would have known our values and seen that it's okay to be sexual. Maybe they wouldn't have been able to get to her."

Priscilla could already feel her eyes starting to tear up. She didn't know what was going on, but she knew it had to be bad.

"Well, what is it? Tell me! Maybe it's not as bad as you think."

Stonefaced, he stared at her.

"Our daughter's a religious fanatic."

9

Today's the day, Josie thought to herself as she and Marcy got out of the car.

"Don't forget the tracts," Josie said as she checked her make up in the side mirror.

"I've got them," Marcy said as she smoothed down her skirt and adjusted her top so her cleavage didn't show that much. She was trying to look somewhat respectable for their first day of witnessing. She and Josie were dressed in their Sunday best. They were wearing short black skirts and conservative white tops. However, Marcy's boobs were just so big that no matter how conservative the top, it was impossible for her to conceal them.

Of course, they had both remembered to wear their black bras and panties. Red wasn't going to be around to see, so they didn't really know why they made this decision. It just seemed like the right thing to do.

"Okay. Let's get started," Josie said breathily as she closed the door to her Nissan.

Never in a million years, would Josie ever have thought that she would be going door to door, handing out tracts and telling people about *The Church of What's Happenin' Now*. While she had come from a fairly conservative background, she and her family had never done anything like this. They had always just gone to church, listened to the service and then gone home. It was just a routine thing for her as a girl. It was a social event more than anything else. This, however, was something else entirely. After she had been healed by Brother Red, she had felt a devotion and love so great that she just knew that she had to be a part of it. She knew that she had to start contributing. She was actually getting involved.

Marcy, on the other hand, had done this sort of thing a zillion times when she was a child. She had grown up a Seventh Day Adventist and had regularly gone around trying to convert and browbeat others to her way of thinking. As a girl, she had routinely chastised meateaters and Sunday keepers as a part of her religious commitment. Of course, she had never really had any sort of freewill in the matter. It was just something that her parents had made her do. So, it was inevitable that once she left home, she had opened her eyes to the fact that most of the people in the world didn't think like her and, as a result, had fallen out of it. She didn't go to church anymore and while she was still a vegetarian, she did enjoy a good cock whenever she could get one. It was just a miracle that she had found a church with so many big cocked men in leadership positions. This had never been the case with the church she grew up in.

After being healed, Josie, along with Marcy and Gunter, had started going to the Cardboard Cathedral on a regular basis. Gunter wasn't really up with the going door to door stuff, though he promised to go a few times just to figure out how to do it. Josie noted that he seemed to be more interested in taking notes of how the operation ran rather than in experiencing the sheer joy that was the Brother Red Hair religious experience. She had also noted that Marcy couldn't keep her eyes above Brother Red's waistline. She wanted a taste of his cock as well, but at least she wasn't so obvious about it.

When they had first started regularly attending, Josie had felt a little guilty about being a porno actress. She wondered if it was right that she was going to church and still fucking on film. Sister Gwen, though, assuaged her fears.

"Josie, I've told you before. It takes all kinds of people to contribute. I'm sure that Brother Red wouldn't want you to change for anything."

Josie was a little relieved. She didn't know what she was going to do if she had to give up her job. After all, she had a car payment and rent to think about.

Red, of course, had already told Sister Gwen that under no circumstances was she to let Josie stop being a porno actress. Sister Gwen was merely waiting for the opportunity to bring it up.

When Josie and Marcy walked about a block up the sidewalk, Josie stopped.

"Well, what about this one?" She pointed to a little A-frame house just to their right.

"I guess it's as good as any," Marcy said and put out her cigarette.

"We can start here and work our way back to the car."

"Okay."

"I'm just so nervous," Josie said as they started walking.

"It's going to be okay. I used to do this kind of thing all the time when I was a kid."

"Oh, yeah, that's right. It's just that I don't want to say the wrong thing or anything," Josie said.

"Well, you remember what Sister Gwen said?"

"Do whatever it takes to get them into church," Josie said.

"Just don't give up too easily," Marcy added. "The biggest thing is getting in the door. That's what they always told us when I was a kid. You can't work on them unless they feel comfortable enough to let you in."

Once at the house, Josie rang the doorbell. No one answered. She rang it again and still no one answered, although they could hear someone, possibly a group of people rustling around.

"Ring it one more time," Marcy said. "If they don't answer, we'll just leave a tract and go to the next house."

Josie nodded. But just as she reached out to ring the doorbell again, the door flew open. Josie and Marcy jumped back in shock.

"What do you want?" A big, muscle bound, tattooed biker type looked wildly out the door. "You ain't the cops, are you? You've got to tell me if you are."

"No…, we're not the cops, we're just spreading the good news," Josie said and tried to smile.

"What do they want?" Another biker type, even bigger than the other one, walked up behind the other type.

"They say they're here to tell us the good news," the first one said.

"Yes," Marcy said, quickly checking out their packages through their dirty, tight jeans. She definitely liked what she saw. "We're here to tell you about Brother Red Hair and *The Church of What's Happenin' Now*. If you just have a minute…"

Suddenly the first biker started grinning and checking her out. "Well, why didn't you ladies say that in the first place."

He opened the door and gestured for them to come in. The second biker type smiled his best smile as well. "Come on in."

Josie looked at Marcy as if to say, do you think we should be doing this?

"Remember what Sister Gwen said. Whatever it takes," Marcy said.

"Yes," Josie repeated. "Whatever it takes."

The two girls walked in and were immediately confronted by the overwhelming smells of sweat, grease, stale beer and marijuana.

"Now, have a seat, girls, and tell us what you want."

Josie and Marcy hesitantly sat down in a broken down loveseat. They could see that in addition to the two bikers who greeted them at the door, there were three more in there as well. They were just as big as the other two. A porno movie played on a brand new big screen TV which was probably stolen.

Marcy nudged Josie. The girl getting fucked on screen was a friend of theirs.

Josie cleared her throat. "What would you do if I said that I could tell you something that would change your life?"

"I would say, let's hear it," the first biker said.

"Okay…" Josie started.

"Hey, hold on a second," the second biker said. "I'm not sure if we're gonna be able to concentrate on what you're saying or not."

"What do you mean?" Marcy said.

"Well, me and the boys were kind of in the middle of watching this here porno movie and I don't know if we're gonna be able to hear about your church. We've got our minds on other things, if you know what I mean." He couldn't help but start grinning.

Josie looked around and saw that all the bikers were nursing enormous hard-ons. She could feel herself getting wet at the very thought of taking on all these guys. She glanced at Marcy, who was already salivating, and could tell that she was thinking the same thing.

"Now, if you girls want to take care of us first, we'll be able to listen to you with a clear head…"

Marcy nudged Josie. "Whatever it takes."

Josie was on her knees and had the second biker's cock out of his pants before he was able to finish talking. Marcy had her skirt off and was over at the three other bikers almost as quick. All the bikers gathered around her as she got down on her knees and started sucking their fully engorged cocks. They were all monster sized, Marcy thought as she attempted to deepthroat the first one. She couldn't wait for them to start fucking her. Meanwhile, Josie had her hands full with the first and second biker. Her head bobbed up and down, going from cock to cock. To be so greasy and dirty looking, the biker's penises were surprisingly clean. She figured that the bikers were more posers than anything else, probably. The bikers looked at each other and couldn't help but smile at their good fortune. Josie was able to bring the pre-cum up fast. She had to slow down or these guys were going to shoot too fast. She couldn't let this day go without being fucked three ways to Sunday by these big dicks.

Slowing the pace down just a bit, so they wouldn't come too quickly, she stood and led the two bikers by the dicks over to where Marcy was servicing the other three. From there she and Marcy swapped places and she was able to get a taste of the other three. After having every dick in her mouth at least twice, the two girls turned up the pace a little bit. They pulled off the rest of their clothes.

"Now, you guys are gonna fuck the living shit out of us. Do you think you can handle that?" Josie said as she rubbed her ass against the first biker.

"I don't think that's gonna be a problem," he said.

Josie grabbed his dick and pulled him down to the floor and guided him into her doggy style. She bucked against him hard and came within seconds. She reached out and grabbed one of the other bikers and sucked him as hard as she could. She could see his eyes rolling back in his head with ecstasy. Marcy, on the other hand was going for the double penetration with two of other bikers while she sucked the other one off. Marcy wailed as she came repeatedly at the double fucking.

"I'm gonna cum!" The second biker said as he pounded into Josie.

"Well, switch with this guy. I don't want to waste any of your cum," Josie said breathlessly. At that, the two bikers switched and she started sucking the second biker while the other aggressively started fucking her, bringing her to another orgasm.

"Oh my God!" the second biker said as Josie began sucking the cum out of his dick. She was like a vacuum cleaner. He came what seemed like a quart and she just kept sucking and swallowing. Pretty soon, the other guy was ready to cum and Josie took care of him in the same way. Then she made her way over to Marcy who was in the process of getting her first load of the day. The biker stood and pumped it into her mouth and as soon as he was finished, Josie went over and French kissed her, taking the snowball into her mouth and swallowing every bit.

She then masturbated as she watched the other two bikers pull out of Marcy and cum simultaneously onto her face. Josie went over to help her clean up, licking and wiping off the cum with her fingers. Josie came again as she swallowed the last bit of jizz.

After they had finished fucking and everyone had their clothes on, Josie and Marcy sat down and told the bikers all about *The Church of What's Happenin' Now*. The bikers listened with rapt attention.

"So, what do you think, fellas? Don't you want to contribute to something good?" Marcy said as she smoothed her skirt and finished the initial presentation.

"Yeah, if you would just go and listen for yourself to what Brother Red has to say, you'll see what we're talking about," Josie said, still savoring the taste of cum in her mouth.

"Do you think you can do us all again?" the second biker said as he started rubbing his penis. "We'll definitely go to church if you do us again."

Josie looked at Marcy. "Well, I am still kind of horny."

"And you remember what Sister Gwen said," Marcy added.

"Whatever it takes," Josie added.

With that, both girls got down on their knees and got to work. Again.

10

Of course, Red was elated after Sister Gwen told him that Josie was already going out and doing the church's work. He had been sure that she would eventually start volunteering, but so soon? Just how good was that? He was positive that it would be no time at all before she was a full fledged member of his staff. Just like Sister Gwen and all the other girls before her. He wasn't that concerned about Marcy. He knew from the way she stared at his cock that she wasn't leaving. It was a definitely a good day at the Cardboard Cathedral. Red felt like his office was going to burst with joy after he heard the news.

"Thank you for the good news, Sister Gwen! Such wonderful news has never come from your mouth."

He gazed at Sister Gwen who looked back at him with a look of sheer joy. She was unable to speak at the time, however, because she had Brother Abernathy's rock hard, big black cock in her mouth. Red was on the vaginal side of a double penetration with Brother Myrtlewood pounding her in her ass. Brother Farlin was taking pictures and jerking off. She convulsed occasionally as she came and took a break from Brother Abernathy's cock to squeal with delight. Dutifully she always went back to sucking. After a bit of this, they switched around, playing musical chairs with her orifices. Red had found that gangbanging Sister Gwen was always good for the morale of the staff. She certainly enjoyed it.

After she came for the umpteenth time, the men were finally ready for some relief. Fucking Sister Gwen was hard but satisfying work and they all deserved a reward. Sister Gwen got down on her knees and gathered all them around her and drained them all. After they had shot their loads into her mouth and she was able to swallow every drop was she able to speak.

"Don't worry, Brother Red," she said as she licked the cum off her lips. "I'll make sure she doesn't quit or get discouraged. And she'll always wear black underwear." She then grabbed Red's penis and sucked him a little more, just to make sure that she had gotten it all.

"Oh, yes!" Red moaned, thinking about Josie in a black bra.

She then did the same with Brother Abernathy and Brother Myrtlewood.

"Oh, yeah, Sister. Oh, yeah," Brother Abernathy moaned as she sucked the remaining drops of cum from his big black penis. She even took Brother Farlin's load, just so he didn't feel left out.

"You did get some good pictures of her deepthroating Brother Abernathy, didn't you?" Brother

Myrtlewood said as Brother Farlin pulled his dick from Sister Gwen's mouth.

"Oh, yeah, I always do."

The purpose of the pictures was to give them something happy to look at whenever life's problems started getting them down. Red was a strong believer in thinking happy thoughts and what best brought about happy thoughts? Happy pictures of course. Of course, he fully trusted that Brother Farlin wouldn't do anything crazy with the pictures like send them to the newspaper or anything.

After they were finished, Brother Abernathy took a small bag of marijuana from his suit pocket and rolled up a joint. He was an expert when it came to marijuana and rolling a joint was his forte. Even with his eyes shut, he could roll one that looked just like a store bought cigarette. He lit it and passed it around. Red took a hit and uncapped the bottle of Canadian Club that he had stashed in his top desk drawer. When it was Myrtlewood's turn with the joint, he was a little slow to pass it back.

"Yo, man, pass that hogleg down to the little lady," Brother Abernathy said.

"Oh, sorry," Brother Myrtlewood said sheepishly and passed it on to Sister Gwen.

"Isn't that the most glorious news you've heard today, brothers?" Red said again, for about the fifteenth time that that evening.

"Red," Brother Abernathy said as he took a hit off the joint. "Just what exactly is so important about this particular girl? I mean, I know it's important to get new members into the church and to get people on the right path, but why the emphasis on her? I mean, if it's a ho you want, they're a dime a dozen."

Red looked at him with a big smile. "I don't want her to be my ho, Brother Abernathy. I want her to be my girlfriend!"

All the people in the room looked at him like he was a little bit crazy at this exclamation. Brother Myrtlewood did a spittake with the Canadian Club.

"Not meaning any disrespect or anything, but don't you think you're kinda going about it in a kind of roundabout way, Red?"

"Yeah, that's what I was thinking," Brother Abernathy said.

Red shook his head and smiled.

Sister Gwen could see through him and was touched.

"Don't you guys see? He wants to impress her. He's just being old-fashioned. I think it's so sweet." She pinched Red on the cheek and he couldn't help but blush.

"She's just so pretty! I just can't for the opportunity to ask her out!"

Brother Abernathy looked at Red a little dubiously. "But don't you think that she might have a problem with all of this?"

"Oh, I don't think so, brother." Red smiled.

"She's a regular little slut," Sister Gwen said matter of factly. "She makes porno films. Nasty ones."

"And that's why I'm so in love with her!" Red beamed.

"She's just so sexy, I just want to eat her up!" Sister Gwen said before she thought about it. Red smiled.

They sat around smoking pot and drinking for about thirty more minutes. Eventually, Brother Abernathy and Brother Myrtlewood began to get a little restless.

"Yo, Red, what time is it?"

Red looked at his Rolex. "It's around midnight."

"Well, I don't know about everybody else, but I think we need to go out and witness to some new females."

"Sounds like a good idea to me," Brother Myrtlewood said. "What about you Farlin?"

"I'm ready."

"How about you Gwen? You want to go pick up some chicks and convert them?"

"Convert them to what?" She purred. "Of course, I'm up for it."

"Red?"

Red smiled at all of them and gently nodded his head. "Do you even have to ask?"

They quickly put on their clothes and headed out to do a little witnessing.

"Strip clubs here we come!" Brother Myrtlewood whooped as they got into Red's Cadillac.

"Don't forget about the massage parlor!" Brother Farlin said, but not before closing his thumb in the door. He hollered as he jerked the thumb back. It didn't look too bad, but he was probably going to lose the thumbnail. He tried his best not to start whining in pain.

"Think you can heal that?" Brother Abernathy said to Red as he examined Brother Farlin's thumb.

They all burst out laughing. Even Brother Farlin.

11

The next week went by like a whirlwind for Josie. She was just brimming over with enthusiasm. She had never been so excited about anything in her life. Not even sex and that was saying something. The odd thing about it was that the zeal she felt for *What's Happenin' Now* and Brother Red Hair carried over to her career too. She was just so much more into her performances than she had ever been before. Having a purpose just made her horny, she supposed. Regardless, she was insatiable on the set. The guys and girls down at *Solid Gold Medallion* couldn't help but comment on it.

"All right, let's have the money shot!" The director barked.

At the moment a stud named Johnny Stiffcock pulled out of Josie's pussy and she got down on her knees and prepared to accept his load. He was big, but she was able to deepthroat him a couple of times before he shot it. He came a lot and she eagerly started deepthroating him again after the camera had captured the initial money shot. She loved it when a guy shot straight into her throat. It was kind of like eating an oyster, she thought. The movie was titled, appropriately enough, *All The Ladies Love Johnny Stiffcock*.

"Damn, girl, what's going on with you? I knew you could suck dick, but damn!" Johnny said breathlessly after the director stopped filming. He couldn't get over how she had just worn him out. She had literally drained him of all his cum and energy. He was exhausted.

Josie licked her lips.

"It's amazing what you can do when you finally figure out what you're put on this earth for." She smiled broadly.

"Well, I definitely know one thing you're good for," the director laughed as he gave her a quick feel. Johnny couldn't help but slap her ass as he moved away.

Solid Gold Medallion was the biggest porn outfits on the west coast, and it was Josie's dream to be one of their contract girls. She was currently a free lancer, shooting for whomever her agent sent her to. Marcy was already a contract girl there and had been trying to get them to pick Josie up for a good while. She knew that Josie would eventually be a contract girl somewhere. She was just too beautiful and sexy not to be. She just hoped that it would be at *Solid Gold*.

Marcy wandered over to Josie from the kitchen. The scene had been shot in the living room of the house. She was still nude from her scene about an hour earlier. She gave Josie a hug and continued to stay close and gently stroked her ass as they talked.

"Do you think they're ready for the tracts?" Josie said excitedly and reciprocated by nuzzling Marcy's big breasts. Those breasts were Josie's biggest weakness, maybe even more so than cock. She didn't know, but she couldn't fathom what it would be like not to be able to touch or kiss them.

"I don't know. I guess we could find out," she began to stroke Josie's pussy as they talked.

"So, what are you girls talking about?" A sexy English voice purred right behind Josie.

It was Vanessa Perkins, a hot new starlet from Britain. She was a sexy and nasty brunette. She was going to be huge.

"Oh, we're talking about our church activities," Josie said breathlessly as Vanessa began to nuzzle her neck and rub her pussy from behind.

The girls were too wrapped up to see that the crew and other actors had all gathered around them and were watching the show. The director silently motioned the cameraman to turn on the camera. He surreptitiously began to film them.

"Sounds brilliant," Vanessa said and got down on her knees and began eating Josie out from behind.

Marcy dropped down to her knees and started eating her out from the front.

"Oh, it is," she said and kissed Vanessa as both girls began to feast on Josie's pussy.

It didn't take Josie long to be overcome by the two girls eating her pussy. She came soon thereafter. After she came, Vanessa and Marcy began fingering themselves. They soon pulled Josie down on the floor and they quickly formed a daisy chain. Marcy licked Josie and Josie licked Vanessa. The room was soon filled by the sounds of the girls moaning in orgasm. The girls were so wet that when Vanessa and Josie began scissoring each other's pussies, they couldn't help but make a smacking sound. Marcy hunched the side of Vanessa's thigh as they all bucked themselves into a full tilt frenzy.

After the girls had all orgasmed, the cast and crew burst into applause. The girls started and finally took a look around them. They started laughing when they saw their audience.

The director walked over to them. "All I've got to say, girls, is that I'm glad we had the camera up."

"You mean you filmed it?" Josie asked.

"Damn straight I did. And don't worry, you'll get paid. You don't get any girl/girl/girl scenes better than that. It was just so intense that I almost jizzed my pants just sitting here."

Josie thought for a second and then whispered something to Marcy, who smiled and nodded her head.

"Instead of paying us with money, there's something else I would like you to do for us."

"Sure, girls, you name it."

Josie smiled.

"Great! This will only take about thirty minutes. Marcy, let's go get the tract literature."

The director looked at Vanessa. She shrugged her shoulders. She didn't have a clue as to what was going on, but she was about to find out.

12

The morning sun was so bright that Red almost had to put on his sunglasses just to think. Maybe it was because he was a little hungover. He didn't know what it was, but even sitting in the middle of the restaurant, everything was bright.

Red put out his cigarette and looked around at the people at his table. If he looked over his plate of eggs and pancakes he could see Brother Abernathy chowing down on a plate full of bacon and eggs. If he looked over his coffee he could see Sister Gwen eating a grapefruit. If he looked under the table, he could not only see up her skirt, he could also see her fingering the blonde stripper sitting next to her. If he continued to look under the table, he could see the stripper giving Brother Myrtlewood a handjob, who was, in turn, fingering another stripper, a brunette. And that brought them full circle around to him. But no, there was someone else, someone sitting right beside him. It was Brother Farlin. He was just sitting there eating oatmeal and staring into space. He was also jerking off.

He looked at all their clothes. They were all rumpled and looked as though they had been slept in, even though there hadn't been any sleeping. Red sighed with satisfaction. This was such a great life. He was so glad that he had started the *The Church of What's Happenin' Now*. He couldn't imagine life any other way. No, wait, there was another way. He could imagine it with Josie by his side. Aside from healing the girl, he didn't know her. However, he had seen enough of her movies to know that he would like her. And he had had the dream. He got hard instantly when he thought about her sitting in his congregation with her black bra and panties.

After they had left the office the night before, they had first tried their luck picking up prostitutes. They managed to get two black girls in the car but were unable to witness to them. After pulling the Cadillac into the parking lot of an electronics store, all the girls wanted to do was suck them all off. They even ate Sister Gwen out.

"I've already got a church," one of them said. "I don't need another one."

"But, baby, this is a different kind of church," Brother Abernathy said breathily as the other one took his massive dick deep in her throat.

"Shut up, moonie and just get yo nut off. I don't want to hear no more." Then she started sucking Brother Myrtlewood. She was like a vacuum cleaner because she had him cumming in a matter of seconds.

The other girl, while enthusiastic, seemed to have a little trouble keeping Brother Abernathy's cock deepthroated for any length of time. Sister Gwen got down there with her and gave her a few pointers.

"Just relax your throat," she said as she took the big black cock in her hands. It was so big that both of her hands didn't even come close to covering it. "Just like this." With that, she took the cock completely down her throat. She had so much of it in her throat that her lips were touching Brother Abernathy's nuts.

"Damn, girl!" the prostitute said. "I can't believe you just deepthroated that big ol'dick. You really know what you're doing."

"I used to be a whore just like you. Until I met Brother Red."

The prostitute looked at her incredulously. Sister Gwen leaned in close to her.

"Brother Red's cock is even bigger than this one," she whispered.

The prostitute looked at Red and couldn't help but smack her lips.

Sister Gwen offered her a tract and the girl took it and put it in her purse. She did it quickly before the other girl, the one who already had a church, could see her.

After taking all of Brother Abernathy's creamy load, she then went to the front seat and started on Red. He was already as hard as a rock.

"Damn, that girl was right about you. I ain't seen too many white boys with a dick this big."

"I'll admit that I've been blessed," Red smiled.

The prostitute went to work and sucked him hard. Using Sister Gwen's technique, she was able to completely deepthroat him up to his balls. Up and down, up and down, she went. She started fingering herself because it was making her so hot. It was obvious that she was wanting it, so when she started tasting precum, she couldn't take any more.

"I'm sorry, but I've just got to get on top of that thang."

"Be my guest, sister."

The prostitute was on top of him in seconds flat. Immediately she started bucking him like she was going crazy. She ground down on him and Red loved every second of it. This girl really knew how to fuck and she was giving him the deluxe treatment. His big cock slid in and out, and she shuddered with orgasms.

"Oh, shit! Goddamn! Shit! Fuck me, you motherfucker!" she yelled during each one. But Red just kept on fucking.

In the back seat, Sister Gwen was being eaten out and watching the action up in the front seat and was cumming so hard that she couldn't see straight. Brother Farlin watched, jerking off, waiting his turn.

"You better cum in my pussy, you motherfucker!" Red's prostitute said.

"If that's what you want."

With that, Red started pumping his spunk into her. He sucked on her big brown titties as he came. When he was finished, the girl got off him and cleaned off his dick with her mouth.

"That was so good, I think I may have to give you a discount."

Red laughed.

"Get that pussy back here!" Sister Gwen hollered as she came. The girl had been munching on her pussy like it was Big Mac extra value meal.

The prostitute went to the back seat and climbed up on Sister Gwen's face. Sister Gwen eagerly ate out all Red's cum from her pussy. And then came again.

"Damn, that's some kinky shit!" The prostitute who had been eating Sister Gwen said as she watched Sister Gwen licking her lips.

After that, the two prostitutes then went to work on Brother Farlin. Within seconds, he blasted his cum over both the girls' faces. This was after they had instructed him to cum in their mouths.

They looked a little pissed off at first, but when Sister Gwen offered to clean it off for them, they calmed down a little.

After that Red tried to witness again, but the girls wouldn't hear any of it.

"Well, pay them out of petty cash then, Brother Farlin."

The girls paid, Brother Red and company went on their way.

Next, they took Red's Cadillac on over to the Va-Va-Voom Room. It was a fairly high class strip club and they were known there. The girls at the club loved

Sister Gwen. They always gave her kisses and free lap dances. Red knew that they would be able to get at least a couple of girls to come to church with them. Several of girls who worked there were already members. They were always more than happy to see Red and his crew.

Several lapdances and trips to the back room later, here they were at the restaurant eating breakfast. The girls were coming over to the office to see what they could do for the church.

And what the church could do for them.

Looking at the two hot girls made Red salivate. The blonde had a body that would stop a clock and the brunette's tits made him ache with horniness. Yes, these girls were going to definitely be favored member of his church. But his mind kept going back to one thing. No matter how much he wanted to get his hands on them, he still wanted to get with Josie even more.

13

"No, baby, I can't drive you and Marcy to the mall," Gunter said very irritably. "I know you want me to join you in handing out the tracts, but I'm sorry I can't go." Then he added as an afterthought, "Besides, if you wanted me to hand out the tracts, why didn't you just say so?"

He paused for a second. "Goodbye. Yes, baby, I will go to the church with you on Sunday."

Gunter sighed. He was a little annoyed that Josie was trying to trick him into handing out Brother Red Hair's tracts, but that wasn't the reason he didn't want to help. No, the reason he wasn't going to drive them wasn't because he didn't want to, but because he couldn't.

"That damn, piece of scheiss Audi!" He bellowed as he looked out his window. Sure, it was a beautiful car and sure it was from the Fatherland, but what good was it him if it was always breaking down? No, that still wasn't the problem. What he meant to think was what good was the car to him if it was always tearing up and he couldn't afford to fix it.

To most people in the porn world, Gunter appeared to be one well to do guy. However, what most people didn't realize was that he was always broke. He was a big star in Europe, he was a big star over here and he wore the nicest clothes and jewelry. Plus, he had that beautiful Audi. All this was true, sure, but the problem was that he spent his money just as fast as he made it. It was like he was a middle man for his money. He was just a conveyance between his employers and his creditors. And yes, while it was great to be recognized on the street, an amazing feat for a porno actor, this sort of thing didn't pay to get the car fixed.

Gunter looked at the two girls stoned and asleep on his couch. They were still there. They fucked him for their room and board and what he called their "spiritual instruction." For a second, he thought about going through their purses to get some money. Then he realized that they probably didn't have any. The problem was that all he needed was some sort of sensor for the car . It probably wouldn't have even cost that much to fix. If he had actually had some money, that is.

He put on his shoes and sauntered on out of the house and down to the corner supermarket. He was all out of baby oil and whipped cream. He hoped he had enough money for those two items. His credit card was maxed out and he was overdrawn at the bank. It would certainly be embarrassing to have to put back two items. Still, it would be good for him to do something to get his mind off that fucking car. He had to come up with a plan. He had a job the next day, but what good was that going to do him now?

When he got to the supermarket, he started to feel a lot calmer. As he picked up his items, he was certain everything was going to work out. Why was he panicking? As he walked through the store, he contemplated buying some beer, but then remembered that he didn't have any money. Then he started panicking again.

"Damn, German piece of shit!" He said aloud.

"You talking to yourself, buddy?"

"Why you..." Gunter said and looked around. He was standing next to the magazine rack. Standing there looking at a porno magazine and rubbing himself through his pants, was a familiar looking old guy.

"Do I know you?" Gunter said, no longer pissed off. His mind was taken off the fact that the guy had smarted off to him by the fact that he was trying to remember who he was.

"I don't know. Do I?" The old man continued to rub himself.

Then it hit Gunter. "I know you, you're from the church. You're Brother..."

"Farlin," the old man said. It was Brother Farlin.

Gunter sidled on over to him like he was his best friend or something. He was still trying to get a handle on the church thing.

"So, tell me, baby, what are you doing here? Shouldn't you be at church doing something for Brother Red?"

Brother Farlin rolled his eyes. "Fuck   Brother   Red. All he wants me to do is take the pictures."

Gunter looked at him curiously. "Pictures?"

"Yeah, I don't always get to join in whenever we gangbang the new girls. Sometimes I can't get my viagra to kick in at the right time. So, I can't get a hard-on when I need to, and by the time it finally gets up, they're all finished. It sucks."

Gunter looked down at Brother Farlin. His dick was making a tent in his pants.

"Yep, the gangbang was over an hour ago."

"That's terrible," Gunter said. His mind was still turning over the statement about the pictures. "So, he makes you take the pictures of the gangbangs, ja?"

"Hell, I take pictures of everything."

Gunter was still puzzled.

"But isn't he afraid that someone may see these pictures?"

Brother Farlin looked at him dubiously. "How would anybody see them. I've got them all stored on my computer at home."

Gunter couldn't think of a thing to say. The cash registers going off in his head were too distracting.

14

Sunday morning finally came and Josie was all a flutter. She was so excited about going to the Cardboard Cathedral that she was on the verge of pissing her pants. She danced around getting ready and modeled about three dresses before she finally decided on a sheer white one. She decided that she liked it best because her black bra and panties could be easily seen through it. Marcy had considerably less trouble. She wore a short black skirt, six inch heels and a white top. She figured that Brother Red would be able to see her black bra through the shirt and his imagination could do the rest.

"Gosh, I'm so excited, Marcy!" Josie said as she brushed her hair for the fifth time. "I don't know what it is, but since I've been going to the Cardboard Cathedral, I'm a new person. You would think I wouldn't still be this excited about going, but it seems I'm more excited than the last time I went."

Marcy nodded. "I know. I can't wait to go either. While I love the sermons, the sight of Brother Red's big dick outlined in those tight pants, just makes the message that much better."

"Oh, I know! And Sister Gwen is so hot!"

"And what about Brother Abernathy! I bet he could throw down on a girl!"

"Yeah, and that Brother Myrtlewood has to be a real freak!" Josie squealed.

"I bet that Brother Farlin is a perv, too." Marcy laughed and put on the rest of her makeup.

Josie sat on the bed and sighed. "I just can't believe that we found such an amazing church. I had almost given up on religion."

After the two girls were ready, they left for church in Marcy's Toyota.

"Don't forget Gunter," Josie said.

"Yeah, his Audi is fucked up again."

"I don't know why he just doesn't buy another one," Josie said and lit up a cigarette. "You know he makes a lot of money."

"I know that he sure knows how to spend it."

They stopped by Gunter's house and honked the horn. Gunter came out about five minutes later, wearing a loose fitting white shirt, tight black jeans and cowboy boots. Again, it looked like he was going to some euro-trash disco. It was obvious that he was from another country.

"Nice outfit," Marcy said sarcastically.

"Thanks, baby. It's my shamen outfit. I think I can focus on the sermon a bit better in it."

Marcy and Josie rolled their eyes.

"Don't you babies think it's cool?" Gunter said as he got into the car.

The girls mumbled something that Gunter took as an affirmative.

After arriving at the church and settling into their seats, Josie took a look around them. Seated all over the church were people from the porn set. Right across the aisle from them she saw Vanessa Perkins and Carmen. She waved at them and they waved back.

"Hey, babies!" Gunter yelled.

Up above them she saw Cedric and just over from him was Jerome. She also saw the director sitting with one of the new starlets.

"I don't know that fucking guy is doing here," Gunter grumbled. "Surely, he isn't thinking that he can start being in the same place as me."

"C'mon, Gunter this is church. What do you have against the director?" Marcy said.

"I don't know. I just don't think he likes the way I fuck. He's an asshole."

Marcy punched him.

Josie took another look around. "Look, Marcy! They're all here! They all listened to us!"

Marcy took a look around and was flabbergasted. She couldn't believe it. They must have made a real impression to get so many people to attend.

Then Josie heard a voice yelling at her from way over on the other side of the building.

"Hey, Josie!"

She looked over and was amazed to see the whole biker gang sitting together. They were wearing clean clothes and everything. Well, they weren't quite clean clothes, but they were cleaner than the ones they had been wearing when the two girls had stopped at their house.

She nudged Marcy and both girls waved at them.

"Well, after a fucking like we gave them, wouldn't you at least be curious about it?" Marcy said matter of factly.

At that time, Brother Myrtlewood started in on the organ like a wildman, making the Hammond jump like a scalded dog. The drummer joined in and pretty soon, people were up and dancing in the aisles and shouting hallelujah. And the service hadn't even started yet. After a few minutes Brother Red ran out and Josie couldn't help but lose her breath for an instant. After he finished smiling and waving at the crowd, Brother Myrtlewood stopped playing. He would only start up again to punctuate Brother Red's comments.

"Brothers and Sisters, I see we've got a lot of new people out there in the congregation today! And to you I just want to say, Welcome! Welcome! Welcome!"

Everybody cheered and erupted into choruses of *Amen!* and *Hallalujah, Brother Red!* Brother Myrtlewood joined in with some crazy organ playing.

Red's eye was immediately drawn to Josie, sitting up in the second tier of the auditorium. He could see her outfit and the black bra and panties through her dress. He got a hard-on instantly. It was obvious through his tight pants. Nothing was left to the imagination. Josie in turn, noticed his hard-on and began to feel her pussy get a little wet. Marcy's mouth began to water. Josie looked over at Vanessa and Carmen and was pleased to see that they both had their skirts up and were very discreetly playing with themselves. She knew that those girls were going to be converted.

After Red got to cranking on the service, it was no holds barred fire and brimstone. He raced through the congregation screaming and shouting. He leaped over the front pews and danced around on the altar. He was like a wild man.

Josie was so stirred by what she saw that she soon found herself screaming *Amen*. It felt good to join in and suddenly she got a strange feeling and she felt the need to get out of her seat. Marcy looked at her like she was crazy, but she just looked around all wild-eyed. The next thing she knew she was dancing in the aisle and before long she was running the aisles just like everyone else. She felt like she was home.

Marcy, however, wasn't quite so moved. She just kept trying to maneuver herself so she could get a better look at Brother Red's cock. Frankly, she was a little amazed at how much Josie was getting into the service, but it was none of her business as far as she was concerned. Gunter, on the other hand, was just taking it all in and continuing to think about what he had talked about with Brother Farlin. He was tempted to wave at Brother Farlin who was sitting glumly down on the front row, but thought that it would probably just look weird.

The service was great and when all the singing and shouting was over, Josie, Gunter and Marcy got out of the seats and went over to Carmen and Vanessa.

"So, what did you think?" Josie asked excitedly.

"I think he has got the sweetest looking dick I have ever seen," Vanessa said.

"I was just oozing thinking about what he could do with that big thing."

Gunter looked at the girls dubiously. "Why are you girls so interested in his dick when you can have mine anytime you want it?"

"Gunter, I *work* with you, I would be fucking him," Vanessa said. "That man's penis is to die for."

"Yeah, they pay us to fuck you. We'd be fucking him for free." Marcy laughed.

"You babies really know how to make a guy feel good about himself," Gunter said sullenly.

"That's great!" Josie said, not paying attention and trying to get the conversation back on topic. "So, do you think you'll be back?"

Carmen and Vanessa looked at her like she was crazy.

"Are you crazy? It's an honor just to be in the same room as a cock like that. Yes, we'll be back, right Carmen?"

Carmen licked her lips. "I can't wait to meet that man."

Josie laughed. "I can't either."

"I think you girls know that I want to do more than meet him." Marcy laughed.

Just then, Sister Gwen came up.

"Sister Gwen!" Josie said excitedly and gave her a big hug. "Vanessa and Carmen, this is Sister Gwen, she was the one who told me about this place."

Sister Gwen put out her hands to the girls.

"You girls work with Josie and Marcy...and this guy?" She winked at Gunter, who winked back in his most suave manner.

"Yep, we're porn sluts, too," Vanessa said.

"Ooh, I love a British accent," Sister Gwen said and licked her lips.

Vanessa was a little taken aback. She had never been come on to by a woman in a church before.

Sister Gwen turned her attention to Josie.

"Josie, Brother Red noticed all the new faces in the crowd today and knows that you're the one who brought them in."

"But how does he know it was me?"

"He had Brother Farlin ask some of them."

"I was just doing what I thought was right. Spreading the good news, you know?" Josie laughed.

"Yes, we know. Well, anyway, Brother Red was so excited about it that he wanted to meet you."

"Well, he has met me. You know when he healed me?" Josie said.

"He knows this. But he wants to actually get to talk to you. He wants to find out more about you. He wants you to come to his office this afternoon.

Josie was flabbergasted. "He wants…me? To come to his office?"

Sister Gwen smiled. "Yes. He wants to personally express his gratitude for your work."

"He probably just wants to fuck you," Gunter said matter of factly.

Everybody ignored him.

"That's great. I'll be there." Josie was so excited that she couldn't think straight. Brother Red was the most positive influence in her life and here she was going to his office. Then she remembered the outline of his penis in his pants. She couldn't help but moisten her lips.

"I helped too. Do I get to meet him?" Marcy asked.

Sister Gwen smiled mischievously. "Brother Red is going to meet with you later. Right now, he wants you to get know Brother Abernathy and Brother Myrtlewood a little better."

Marcy was wet instantly.

"So, if we help, can we meet him, too?" Carmen said, fidgeting a little. Her pussy was so wet at the thought of Josie fucking Brother Red that she just couldn't stand still.

"Of course. Brother Red always has time to meet sincere young ladies such as yourself."

"Well, count us in," Vanessa said. "Whatever it takes, we'll do it."

"Okay," Sister Gwen smiled. "First of all, you can come back to my office and I'll get you set up." She winked at the two girls then she turned to Josie. "Be there at one o'clock. He's dying to meet you."

Josie gulped and nodded. She couldn't wait.

"But what about me? Don't I get to go back to your office too?" Gunter said as everybody was walking off.

"I guess you're on your own, this time, Fritz," Sister Gwen said.

Gunter grumbled a little bit under his breath as everybody walked off, but then he saw Brother Farlin. Maybe he wasn't going to be on his own, after all.

15

"**G**ood Lord! There she is! On TV!" Hal said as he excitedly jumped up and ran over to the television. He had been in the process of getting a blowjob from Jenny while sitting in a recliner over at Bob and Jenny's place. They lived in a split level in the adjoining subdivision. It was decorated in a very cool seventies style on the inside, with lots of heavy wood and a neo-medieval feel.

Jenny, needless to say, was a little confused. She had been about to finger herself to orgasm when Hal had jumped up from his blowjob.

"Who?"

Priscilla looked up from looked up from the floor. She was in the process of getting it doggie style from Bob.

"It's Josie! She's running the aisles! At that church!"

Bob just kept pumping, sliding his penis in and out of Priscilla's engorged vagina. The two of them didn't miss a beat as Priscilla turned her attention to the screen.

"I can't believe it! It's even worse than a cult! She's following a fundamentalist!"

"C'mon, Hal," Jenny said as she walked over to him. She got down on her knees and returned to sucking on his still hard penis. "Surely, it's not as bad as you think," she said as she took a breath.

"Oh, it is. She just wasn't raised this way," Hal said as he rubbed Jenny's head and pushed her mouth down further onto his dick. "She was raised an Episcopalian, wasn't she, hon?" He looked at the TV again and saw Red up there on stage, jumping around and clapping his hands. "And just who the hell is that red-headed bastard?"

Priscilla's eyes were rolling back in her head at the pounding she was receiving from Bob.

"She's gonna be completely screwed up now," she groaned and rubbed her clit. "Fuck me harder, Bob!"

Bob picked up the pace and slapped her on the ass.

Jenny turned away from Hal's dick and was now presenting her pussy to him. He stuck one finger in her asshole and then stuck his dick in her pussy all the way up to his balls.

"Oh, God, yes!" Jenny shrieked as Hal began to piston her.

Even as he fucked, Hal still couldn't take his eyes off Josie who was shaking and convulsing to the crazy organ music. It was just almost too much for him to handle. Luckily for him though, Jenny was just so damned hot that nothing could deter him from fucking her.

Priscilla was clawing the carpet as Bob pumped her hard. She hadn't been fucked like this since the last time he had fucked her. Bob was no spring chicken, but he fucked better than most guys half his age. He was around forty, so the math was pretty easy. She marked it up to experience. He was almost as good as the black kid down at the paint store. She had repainted the entire house twice because of him. She just couldn't get enough of his jizz. She had even considered freezing some of it, to have whenever she started feeling horny, but she realized that people might think she was a little crazy and decided not to do it.

"God, I'm gonna cum!" Priscilla said suddenly and she started rubbing her clit like crazy. Bob kicked it into high gear. In and out, he thrusted as her body began to shake. The rhythm of his thrusts matched that of her moans as she squirted all over his dick.

After she was finished, he decided that he couldn't hold it any more, so he pulled out. Priscilla eagerly took it in her mouth and began to suck as he started to cum. Bob always came huge amounts and today was no exception. She clamped her lips around his dick and began to gulp his semen as he pumped the massive load into her mouth. She didn't waste as single drop.

Jenny glanced over and was relieved that none had fallen onto her new carpet. But then she noticed that Priscilla had squirted everywhere. She couldn't help but reach down and start rubbing her pussy at the thought of it.

After witnessing the major fucking going on between her husband and Priscilla, Jenny picked up the pace and started bucking against Hal like a wild animal. He responded in kind and began fucking her so hard that she thought her fillings in her teeth were going to come loose. She loved to be fucked hard like this and started to cum instantly.

"Harder! You motherfucker!" She screamed and reached back and slapped Hal on the ass. "C'mon!"

Hal picked up the pace and began to really give her even harder. Pretty soon she settled down and he knew that she was finished. He decided to go ahead and cum.

"Where do you want it, Jenny?"

Jenny looked back at him and grinned. "I want it in my pussy. I want you to fill me full!"

Hal ejaculated deep into Jenny's vagina as he pumped her. He felt like he hadn't cum in ages as he filled her full to the rim. After he pulled out, he reached down and scooped up a couple of fingers' worth. Jenny grabbed his hand and sucked the semen off. She reached down and got some herself and began to eat it as she masturbated herself to another orgasm with the other hand.

Hal grinned, but then he saw the television again. His face fell. He looked over at Priscilla and saw that she had the same expression. Behind her, Bob poured gin and tonics for everyone. They were definitely going to need a drink.

"We're gonna have to do something," Priscilla said and lit a cigarette. The two nude couples sat on the floor and relaxed as scenes of Josie reaching religious ecstasy filled the screen.

"Why don't you two go out there?" Jenny said and went over to Priscilla.

"Yeah, you could go out there and try to talk some sense into her," Bob said as he handed everyone their drinks.

"But she'll hate us, don't you think?" Priscilla said.

Hal put his head in his hand. "I knew we should have told her about us. About the *Lifestyle*. Maybe she wouldn't have done this."

"Oh, c'mon, Hal," Jenny said and took a sip of her drink. "You don't know that."

"At least if she had joined a cult, we could have her deprogrammed," Hal said.

Bob got a quizzical expression on his face. "Who says you can't still do that?"

"What do you mean, Bob?" Priscilla said, growing interested.

"Well, we could all fly out there and talk to her. We could tell her about our Lifestyle and how joining a religious group like that will ruin her career…"

Hal snapped his fingers. "Her career. Yeah, that's it. She loves being a porno actress. She obviously hasn't thought this thing through otherwise she would know that those people are going to make her stop."

Jenny chimed in, "Yeah, you can tell her about swinging and how it's ok to fuck other people and maybe she'll see just how crazy this religion stuff is."

Priscilla got a very determined expression on her face. "That does it. We're all flying out tomorrow and we're going to deprogram her."

"I'll book the flight right now," Bob said.

"If she could just see what she's doing with her life," Hal said, wringing his hands.

"Well, I guess we need to get packed," Jenny said and stood up.

"Jenny, one thing, don't forget your double headed dildo," Priscilla said.

Jenny gave her an odd look. "Priscilla, this is your daughter we're talking about, remember?"

Priscilla rolled her eyes. "It's not for her. It's for us. I know I'm gonna have to relieve some tension before this is over."

16

As she was ushered back though the winding, utilitarian-looking hallway to Brother Red's office, Josie could feel herself growing so excited that she was about to jump out of her skin. She was so wet she was dripping. The thought of being alone in a room with Brother Red and his massive cock was just almost too much to think about.

Meanwhile, Red sat in his office, awaiting Josie's visit with so much excitement that his tight pants were about to split from the enormous hard-on he was sporting. He absently minded stroked his penis through his pants, fantasizing about Josie wearing the black bra and panties. He was truly in love with her and he couldn't wait to give her the fucking of her life. He picked up a cream-filled doughnut from a box on his desk. He bit in and wondered if it was too soon to propose. After all, that was his ultimate goal. He had been with scads of women and had never been moved to such an extent as he had by watching Josie's movies. He just hoped that his brain would be able to function once he saw her in real life. Josie was the red-headed slut of his dreams and he did not want to blow it. He didn't, for one moment, doubt that she would be the wanton woman he so desired.

Red was just finishing his doughnut when Josie knocked on his door. He hurried up and swallowed. He checked himself in the mirror before he got the door.

"Hello, Miss Bistro," Red said coolly as he opened the door.

Josie's breath was taken away. Brother Red was even more good looking than she remembered and that cock! It was so huge! He was making no attempt to hide his hard-on.

"Hello…" Josie hesitated. She didn't know how exactly to address a man of Brother Red's stature.

"Just call me Red," Red laughed. "Please come in and have a seat."

Josie giggled and went in. Red bit his lip when Josie walked past him. Her ass was just so scrumptious that he could feel himself almost on the verge of cumming just from looking at it.

Josie sat down in a comfortable leather chair across from his desk. Red sat down on the desk in front her.

"Do you want a doughnut?" Red offered her the box.

Josie declined. "No, thanks, I just ate."

Red placed the doughnuts back down on the desk and was suddenly at a loss for words. What can you say when the woman of your dreams walks through your door? Josie nervously looked around the room for a few seconds not knowing if she was going to be kicked out of the church or what. She noticed that the office was decorated with ancient scrolls and also some phallic looking fertility statues. She was impressed. Finally, Red realized that he had to say something or he was definitely going to lose her attention.

"Miss Bistro…" Red began.

"You can call me Josie," Josie giggled. "I don't mind."

Red almost swooned.

"Josie," he smiled. "You're probably wondering why I asked you to come here."

"Sorta."

"Well, one of the reasons is that I really appreciate all the work you're doing for the church. You are, indeed, a blessing."

"Thanks, Red," Josie beamed. "I love helping out. I tell you, coming to the Cardboard Cathedral has been one the best things that's ever happened to me."

"Thank you, sister. Thank you," Red said and leaned in a little closer to her. He got a better look at her cleavage and his hard-on jumped. It was almost too much just looking at her bra and panties through her see-through dress, but this was something else entirely. Josie breathing sped up as his still hard monster dick moved closer to her. "Actually, there's another reason I wanted you to come to my office."

Before he had a chance to say anything, Josie suddenly got a thought.

"You don't want me to quit being a porno actress do you?" Josie blurted out, her heart sinking. She didn't know what she would do if he asked her to do that. She had asked Sister Gwen this question before, but for some reason, was never satisfied with her answer. She wanted to find out from the man himself.

Red started chuckling. "No, no, sister. We've got room for all God's children here. No, it's nothing like that at all." Red smiled. "It's just that…" Red hesitated. "I think you are absolutely the most beautiful woman I have ever seen and I would love it if you would go out with me tonight."

Josie's breath was taken away. She just couldn't believe her ears. Brother Red Hair and his cock had just asked her out!

Without hesitating or even giving it any thought, Josie answered, "I would love it!"

Red burst into a smile and almost started dancing around the room. He was so happy. Josie, on the other hand, couldn't keep her eyes off his massive penis. It was like it was mesmerizing her to a point where she felt like she was yearning for it. Before she realized it, she found her talking.

"But only on one condition."

Red's smile fell. What if she wanted something that he couldn't possibly give her? Surely, it wasn't supposed to end this way?

"You've got to let me have a taste of that big cock of yours," Josie said before she thought about it.

Red looked at her a bit strangely. "You want what?" He said and broke into a grin.

Josie put her hand over her moutht. Surely, she didn't just say that.

"Oh, I'm so sorry! I can't believe I just said that! Please forget what I just said! I'm a porno actress, remember? I just can't keep my filthy mouth shut!" Josie was so embarrassed that wanted to run from the room.

Red leaned in close to her and started rubbing her breasts.

"I think I can meet your condition," he said and started nuzzling her neck. Josie moaned as her hands immediately went to Red's zipper. The big dick sprung out of his pants and she had in her mouth in no time. She got down on her knees and started sucking for all she was worth. Red again looked down her top at her tits, still encased in her black bra and felt himself starting to lose control. He put his mind on something else and began to push her head down, driving his cock down her throat. He was there fast. At the first taste of Red's salty pre-cum, Josie began to finger her already wet pussy through her panties. She orgasmed within seconds and was well on her way to another one when Red gently took his dick out of her mouth and hoisted her up onto his desk and began to eat her out. She came again as he began to munch on her delicious pussy. His face was soon coated with her juice, but he kept licking and sucking and driving her crazy. He stuck one finger up her ass as he licked. While she loved the way he ate pussy, she really wanted to have that big dick of his inside of her.

"C'mon, Red, fuck me," she moaned breathily as she rolled over onto her stomach.

He stood up and gently put it in, going just an inch at a time until he was finally all the way in. He was amazed that such a little girl was able to take his full eleven inches so easily. There had been very few that could.

Looking down at her sweet ass and at her beautiful tits squashed down on the desk top, Red was inspired to start fucking her hard. She looked like she needed a good hard fucking. It was what she was used to. Anything less than a ferocious pounding would be a letdown to a girl like her. He almost started cumming just thinking about all the men that she had been with and how easily that she allowed men to fuck her. His dream girl was a slut and he couldn't have been happier.

"Give it to me, Red! Harder!" Josie moaned as she convulsed with another orgasm. She bucked against him harder and harder until he was certain that they were actually moving the heavy mahogany desk. He threw it into high gear. After that, he couldn't stand it anymore.

"I'm gonna cum!"

Josie got down on her knees and started giving him head. She licked the tip of his big cock until he finally squirted all into her mouth and all over her face. As she wiped the sperm from her face with her fingers, she realized that she had never seen a man cum so much. She licked her fingers and realized that Red not only had an enormous cock, but he also was full of cum. How did she get so lucky? She asked herself.

Red sat down on his desk and lit a cigarette for himself and Josie. As they smoked, they just looked at each other and couldn't stop smiling.

"Are you sure you don't want a doughnut?" Red asked again.

"Thanks, Red. I've changed my mind. I think I would like one."

17

Brother Farlin lit up a cigarette in the hallway that contained the church offices. He was pretty aggravated. He had just finished talking to that guy, Gunter, and was now a little pissed off. How dare that guy think that he would betray the only man who had ever given him a chance just for a little pocket money and revenge.

"That guy deserves to burn in hell," Brother Farlin mumbled to himself as he walked past Brother Red's office. He had taken his Viagra in anticipation of banging the girls, but, for some reason, had not been invited to any of the activity. He thought for a second about knocking on Brother Red's door, but then realized that it probably wasn't a good idea. That girl, Josie, was something special to him. While he knew that Brother Red might not mind sharing her, he thought it best to wait until the girl was actually presented to them. He didn't want to be rude or anything. He knew that Red would start sharing her eventually. He couldn't help but feel a small twinge in his penis and lick his lips in anticipation.

He walked on down the hall, ashing his cigarette in a potted plant. His hard-on was aching at the thought of Josie getting fucked by Brother Red. He could just imagine her clawing the floors while she was getting it hard from behind. He just couldn't hardly stand it. He started rubbing himself through his pants. He then heard some animal-like grunting coming from the office directly in front of him. He paused for a second and then realized that Brother Abernathy and Brother Myrtlewood were servicing Marcy! How could he have forgotten that? Now, that girl was a real piece of ass. He guessed it was because that guy Gunter was muddling his mind. What kind of a person did that guy take him for, anyway? That guy didn't know him. He wasn't even an American for God's sake!

He walked into the office and was pleasantly surprised to see Marcy being sandwiched by Brother Abernathy and Brother Myrtlewood. Brother Abernathy was dogging her and Brother Myrtlewood had his dick stuck deep down into her throat. Her enormous breasts heaved with every thrust she gave and took. Her leg muscles were taut as she received her pounding from Brother Abernathy.

Brother Farlin couldn't help but break into a smile. His erection was already straining his pants. It begged for release. He started taking his pants off when Brother Abernathy noticed him.

"Yo, Farlin, go get the camera, man! We've got to go get some pictures of this."

"Yeah, man, get the pictures! This girl is crazy!" Brother Myrtlewood turned and chimed in. Marcy almost started laughing, but was unable to due to the large dick in her mouth.

"Oh, we don't need the camera, do we?" Brother Farlin almost whined. "I want to get some too."

Marcy looked up and took the dick out of her mouth long enough to talk. "C'mon, Brother Farlin, take some pictures. You can jerk off while we fuck. I love to see a man jerk off while I'm getting fucked." Then she suddenly started bucking against Brother Abernathy as she had a monstrous orgasm.

"I think I'm losing my mind!" She said as she came.

Brother Abernathy picked up the pace and started really long-stroking her. "You heard her, man! Go get it!"

Brother Farlin just stood there and started rubbing his dick. Then he decided to go get the camera.

A couple of seconds after he had left, Brother Myrtlewood pulled out of her mouth.

"I can't stand it no more!" He said and started shooting his load all over her face and tits. She opened her mouth and lapped up the cum like she hadn't had anything to eat in days. Brother Abernathy almost lost it when she began licking the semen off her breasts.

"C'mon, hurry up, Brother Abernathy, I want some of that black cum on me too!" Marcy said breathlessly as she turned around.

"Yeah, baby!"

Brother Abernathy pulled out and unloaded into her waiting mouth.

Brother Farlin came back with the camera a couple of minutes later. He started masturbating again and then noticed that everyone was sitting around smoking cigarettes. He also noticed that Marcy was coated in cum.

"You're too late, brother. You missed it," Brother Abernathy said as he took a long drag off his Kool.

"I'm sorry," Marcy said sheepishly. "I really wanted to give you a good show. We just got too worked up."

Brother Farlin put the camera down and stood there for a minute, stroking his hard-on but not really getting anything out of it. He was a little miffed that they hadn't waited on him. He thought for a second and walked out. He didn't want to say anything that he might regret later. He walked down the hallway, hard-on in hand, wondering how in the world that his so-called friends could be so rude to him. He didn't ask for much. He just wanted to get a piece of the action too. He was on the verge of getting depressed when all of a sudden he heard some moans coming out of Sister Gwen's office. That was good news. Sister Gwen was a real party girl and would fuck almost anything that moved. Maybe she would be able to do something about his aching hard-on.

He opened the door quietly, hoping maybe to get a glimpse of the action before anyone knew he was there. He slipped in unnoticed and was astounded by what he saw. Sister Gwen was on the one side of a double headed dildo with a girl, who from her moans, sounded English. It was Vanessa. His penis really stood to attention when he saw Sister Gwen's face buried in a beautiful Latina's pussy. It was Carmen. Sister Gwen was showing them the ropes all right.

Sister Gwen was really munching too. Carmen sat in an office chair and had her fingers buried deep in her hair and held her head tight as she hunched against her face. Vanessa soon pulled the double headed dildo out. She licked it first and then began eating Sister Gwen. It was a daisy chain. Vanessa ate vigorously, and fingered her own pussy while she licked. The girls moaning occasionally reached feverish pitches as they came.

Brother Farlin stood there for a second really giving it all he had, feeling the semen welling up inside of him. As he watched the girls having sex, it was almost overwhelming for him. The smell of pussy was just so strong. He stepped out into the room, hard-on displayed for the girls to see. He had to have a piece and he had to have it now!

Vanessa screamed when she saw him.

"AAAAhhhh! Who's that pervert!"

Carmen jumped about a mile off the chair and Sister Gwen quickly turned to see what was the matter.

"Brother Farlin! You shouldn't be sneaking around like that!"

"I just couldn't help myself."

"You know him?" Carmen said, pointing at him like he was some sort of thing.

Sister Gwen quickly explained who Brother Farlin was and the girls breathed a sigh of relief. Pretty soon, they were getting frisky again and Brother Farlin moved in closer to the action. Maybe he would be able to get some from Sister Gwen at least.

As he started sucking on Sister Gwen's sweaty tits, she sat up.

"I've got a great idea!" She turned to Brother Farlin. "Why don't you go get the camera?"

Brother Farlin looked at her like he could've fallen through the floor.

"That's a brilliant idea!" Vanessa chimed in.

Carmen nodded her head enthusiastically.

Brother Farlin looked at them and then sighed. He picked up his pants and walked out the door and towards his office. He wasn't going to get the camera, however he was going to make a phone call.

18

"Gosh, I just don't know if I can believe all this," Josie said as she sat across from Red at the Chateau Gourmet that Sunday night. It had once been one of the swankiest eateries in Red's part of Los Angeles. It was decorated with heavy drapes and dark wood and had been around since the forties with little or no remodeling. Some people might have called it a dump but to Red it was very stylish. It had a lot of character, he thought. Looking over at Josie in her sheer black dress, he was still amazed at how lucky he was.

"C'mon, Josie. Surely, that doesn't blow you away you that much," Red said as he took a sip of his wine. He wasn't even looking over his shoulder as he drank. He usually did to watch for snoops sent out by the other televangelists. It was a very cutthroat business and he always had to be on his toes. If any one of them saw him drink or be out with a girl like Josie, it would be reported directly to their superiors and the war would be on. This was especially true of his arch rival, the Reverend Simon Pure. That guy was always trying to get him on something.

"But, Red, you're a preacher! Preachers don't go around screwing anyone they want to. It's like you're a…swinger or something."

Red had opened up and told Josie about his philosophy of free love and how one shouldn't be ashamed to get down and freaky however and with whoever one likes. Josie, needless to say, was a little taken aback. She had never met a preacher like this before. She didn't know what to think, but she was thinking that she liked it.

"Josie, I believe that sex between two or more consenting adults is a beautiful thing. It's just people being people. Besides, it's just fun. I don't see anything morally wrong with it all."

Josie looked at him over her lobster for a minute and then smiled.

"So, is that why you don't mind me being a porno actress?"

Red smiled. "Well, sort of, but there's more…" He debated with himself for a moment whether or not to tell her his dream. It was early and it was only their first date. He decided against it. There would be time later. "I just think that you're a great porno actress and it would be a shame for you not to do something you love and are good at."

Josie swallowed her lobster and took a sip of wine. "You're right about that. I love it. Getting fucked by guy or girl I've only known for a few minutes is one of the biggest turn-ons I can think of." Josie paused and thought for a second. "So, you really don't mind that I'm porno actress? I'm not talking about the church, I'm talking about…as far as we're concerned."

Red smiled. "I just want you to be happy."

Josie smiled and took another bite of lobster.

After they finished dinner, Red drove Josie around to some of his charities. Most were in the rougher parts of town. They were usually in partially abandoned strip malls and shopping centers. They drove by thrift stores, soup kitchens and literacy centers.

"Wow, you do so much good, Red. It's such a turn-on to be around somebody who impacts so many people's lives."

"I'm just a tool. Remember that. If I don't help people, I don't think that I'm doing what I'm supposed to be doing." This was probably the most true thing about Red. He always believed in sharing. Whether it came to his money or his women, what was his was everybody else's. Everybody deserved a piece. While he realized that he was a little over the top and sometimes acted as though he had a little more power than he really did, he also realized what he did was for the greater good. If people bought it and it made their lives a little easier, then so be it.

"That's so sweet," Josie said and gave him a little kiss. She rubbed his crotch through his pants and was pleased to see that he was already hard. She lingered on the head for a minute, still amazed at its enormity.

"There's another place I want to show you," Red said and did a u-turn

He drove for a couple of minutes, deeper into the bad part of town.

"It's just up there." Red pointed up ahead at a lighted building. It was the only building with lights in the whole deserted industrial block. Besides the building, there was nothing on the street but abandoned warehouses and train tracks. They pulled up to it and parked on the street, in front.

"It's a mission house," Josie said.

"Yep, this is where I started out. This is the birthplace of the Cardboard Cathedral, even before there was a *Church of What's Happenin' Now.*"

When they walked in, they were greeted to lots of "hellos" and handshakes. People gathered around Red like moths to a flame. There were old people, young people and all sorts of people in between. Josie was very impressed, even though it saddened her to see the poverty etched on the people's faces. Regardless, it was easy to see that these people loved Red. The place was just a big room filled with cots and only had a small kitchen. Still, though, it was the only home that some of them had known for years.

A big, long haired Mexican looking guy wearing an apron walked up to Red and gave him a hug.

"Red! It's so good to see you, brother!"

Red hugged him back. "This here is Brother Juan. He runs the place."

Brother Juan extended his hand. As Josie took it, she couldn't help but notice what a stud he was. He was muscular and she could see everything through his tight jeans. He was hung like a horse. Not as big as Red, but still, who was?

"Pleased to meet you," Juan said. "Any friend of Red's is a friend of mine." Just then there was a little ruckus in the back of the mission. "If you'll excuse me for a second, I have to go take care of some trouble." He walked quickly to the back for a second. It appeared that a midget was wrestling with an old woman for a cot.

"Juan here was one of the worst crack heads I've ever seen. But he's really straightened himself up and now he's in charge of the place."

"Wow, that's great," Josie said.

"All he needed was a chance," Red said.

Josie looked at Red for a second. "Red, I want to help. What can I do?"

Red looked at her for a minute. "Well, I'm sure Juan needs some help in the kitchen. Maybe we could go back there…"

"But I'm no good in the kitchen!" Josie whined. "I'm no good at anything."

Red thought for a second and smiled. "Well, you are good at something, you know."

Josie thought for a second and smiled.

She grabbed Red by the hand and walked to the kitchen. Brother Juan came in few seconds later.

"Man, that midget is always starting something!" Brother Juan said and washed his hands.

"Juan, I want to help," Josie said and moved in close to him.

"Well…" Brother Juan said at a loss for words. "I don't really need…"

"No, Juan, she insists," Red said and smiled and started rubbing Josie's ass.

Brother Juan smiled as Josie pulled his penis out of his pants. She got down on her knees and clamped her lips onto the head. He grew hard as she sucked and within seconds he was fully upright. Red pulled out his dick and began to rub it. It had been hard all night and it felt good to finally give it a little attention. He lifted up Josie's skirt and was a little disappointed to see that she wasn't wearing any panties. Still, an ass like that was nothing to sneeze at.

She unbuttoned her dress as she sucked and pushed it down around her waist. She was wearing a black bra. Delighted, Red almost moaned at the sight of it. He got down and began to lick her pussy as she sucked Juan's dick. She tasted great and was so wet that she was dripping onto the floor. Soon, his face was glazed over. He couldn't wait any longer. The sight of the woman of his dreams slutting herself out to another man was just too much for him. He pulled down his pants and put his big dick in her. She shuddered with excitement as he began to stroke her doggie style. Red was amazed. He hadn't even started fucking her good yet and she had already had an orgasm. She continued to suck

Brother Juan and soon she could taste the pre-cum. She began to rub her tits and the combination of the taste and Red's hammering her pussy, she came again. Red really started pumping her then. Brother Juan had hard time fighting the urge to cum, but somehow he managed.

"I've got to fuck you in the ass, girl!" Brother Juan said breathily.

"I would love that!" Josie said as she took a breath.

Red smiled and changed places with Juan. This time Josie was on all fours and giving head to Red while Brother Juan began to insert his dick into her anus. He rubbed her pussy as he did it. At first, he thought that it might be a little tight, but to his surprise, he slid right in.

"Damn! This girl is off the hook!" Brother Juan said happily and began to ream her.

Josie laughed and then started deepthroating Red. After a little bit of Juan's pounding she had the biggest orgasm of the night. Anal orgasms were always big for her but this time, she almost drew blood from Red's legs she was clawing them so hard. She was lucky that her screams of ecstasy didn't bring draw an audience.

After she had finished shaking and convulsing, it was all that Red could take. He pulled out and shot cum all over her face and in her mouth. Before she even had a chance to lick it up, Brother Juan came with a shudder all over her ass.

Josie wiped up the cum and licked her fingers clean.

Brother Juan just looked at her in amazement. "You can come and help me anytime!" He laughed and high-fived Red.

Josie just laughed, but couldn't help but notice the odd smile on Red's face. She didn't know it, but he was the happiest man on Earth at that moment. He had also decided to tell her his dream.

19

"God, I've got to have a cigarette!" Priscilla said after their plane landed in Atlanta. They had a two hour layover before the second leg of their flight to Los Angeles took off.

Jenny gave Priscilla an odd look. "You don't smoke!"

"After a flight like that I do," Priscilla said as they trucked their way into the concourse. The turbulence had been so bad that, at one point, Priscilla's head had bumped the overhead bin.

"It was great that we were able to get these tickets on such short notice," Hal said, hustling to keep up with Priscilla.

"Don't be too thankful. We did have to stop in Atlanta," Bob said.

"Oh yeah."

They hurried along and finally went into a smoking lounge that adjoined a bar. Bob and Hal went to buy some beer while the girls lit up.

"I only hope that we're not too late," Priscilla said, savoring the Marlboro Ultra Light. It was the first one she had had in over five years. It was a little harsh but it tasted good.

"I'm sure we're not. Josie's a smart girl. She can make up her own mind."

"I hope so," Priscilla exhaled.

After a few minutes the guys came back with the beers. Everyone was so thirsty, that they looked like about most refreshing things in the world. After about half a glass, the girls began feeling a little tipsy.

"You're not gonna believe this but I think I'm feeling a little drunk," Jenny said.

"You and me both," Priscilla said.

Bob and Hal laughed and talked about the news that was showing on the smoke room's television.

Jenny looked around the smoking lounge. There weren't a lot of people, just a few workers and some foreigners. Then she looked at Priscilla slyly. She moved her chair closer to her.

"What are you doing?" Priscilla said.

"Ssshh," Jenny said as she slipped her hand up Priscilla's denim skirt. She found her mark within seconds and began to gently massage Priscilla's pussy.

"Mmmm…" Pricilla moaned. "What are you doing?"

"I'm relieving some of your stress." Jenny said as she kept rubbing. After Priscilla was good and juicy, she licked her fingers, but not before offering them to Priscilla who eagerly tasted herself.

Bob nudged Hal and pointed over to the girls. Hal couldn't help but start grinning. Only someone who was actually paying attention to them could have been able to see what was going on. It just looked like the two women were sitting together. Bob and Hal blocked any clear view of what was going on.

Jenny slipped three fingers into her pussy and began to gently finger fuck her. She moved them in a small circular movement. This clearly did the trick. Priscilla writhed and after a few minutes began to cum. She stifled the urge to cry out in ecstasy. However, she did cum with an enormous shudder.

After she came, she lit a cigarette and gave Jenny a deep french-kiss.

"Me next," Hal joked to Jenny.

"Well, come on over and let's get started," Jenny said.

"Shut up," Priscilla said suddenly.

Everyone at the table looked at her a little odd. Surely, she wasn't picking this moment to be jealous.

"I didn't offend you by saying that to him did I?" Jenny asked nervously.

"No. Don't be silly. Look," Priscilla said and pointed at the TV.

They all turned and looked at the screen. The smiling face of Brother Red Hair filled the screen. It was a report about an alleged sex scandal at *The Church of What's Happenin' Now*.

Red's little secret was out. All the tales and pictures of his debaucheries had hit the news. The report mentioned that he was into group sex, prostitution, porn and many other sexual perversions. Of course, most of what was being said was pure fabrication, but it's irrelevant to most people whether or not something is true or not, just that somebody says it. The reporter even spoke to Red's rival, the Reverend Simon Pure.

"This man deserves nothing less than hell!" The Reverend Pure thundered as his face turned red and the veins popped out in his head. "The problem today is that there's no accountability! There's no consequences! Well, there's gonna be consequences in hell for Red Hair, I can guarantee that!"

"We've got to hurry," Priscilla said. "There's no telling what kind of depraved person Josie has decided to follow."

"Why that pervert!" Hal said. "Just wait until I get my hands on him!"

20

"I...just...don't know what to say." Josie was speechless. She was lying nude on Red's bed, trying to keep her legs from turning to jelly. She smoked a cigarette and focused her attention on Red's giant cock which was still semi hard even after having sex with her all night.

Red's mansion was out in the suburbs. It was an extravagant house that had once belonged to some silent movie mogul who had gotten into trouble for being married to three women at the same time. It was gigantic and Red had decorated it so that it was more suited for European royalty than it was a fundamentalist preacher from Texas. It was very high on the gilt and velvet and very low on the modesty. It was like Elvis Presley and Marilyn Monroe had run amok.

"Don't say anything. I just wanted you to know just how special you are to me," Red said. He focused on her gorgeous breasts in an effort not to appear too nervous. He had just told her his dream about them being married. He had told her everything from the gangbang to the black bra and panties. He had told her how much he loved slutty women and exactly how much she meant to him. He had been extremely nervous about doing it, but he felt that he had to. He was just so happy and he wanted her to know that she was the one for him.

"That's just so romantic," Josie said, reaching out and stroking Red's cock with her free hand. The other hand ashed the cigarette into an ornate jade ashtray that Red had picked up on one of his many crusades to Southeast Asia. She just didn't know what to say. She was so moved that she almost wanted to burst into tears. As far as she knew she had never been the girl of anyone's dreams. Then she remembered that she was a porno actress and realized that she probably had, but, regardless, she had hit the jackpot with this one. To be the girl of a great man like the Brother Red Hair's dreams was something she had never thought possible. It was like she was Cinderella or something. It was like the man of her dreams had picked her. It was overwhelming. Her eyes began to well up with tears.

Red moved in close and kissed her. "What's wrong? I didn't scare you or anything, did I?"

"Red," Josie said, breaking into a smile, her eyes still teary. "That's the sweetest thing anything anyone has ever said to me. I'm so lucky to have you."

Red was so happy. His dreams had come true and his prayers had been answered. He leaned over and began to kiss Josie deeply. She kissed him back and began to gently stroke his penis. He stiffened instantly. He reached down and began to rub her pussy. It was still a little raw from the workout he had given her earlier, but she was already wet to the touch.

"Red, let's skip all this stuff and get down to the fucking," Josie said breathily as he put his fingers into her. Her breasts heaved up and down in her excitement.

Red broke into a smile. He leaned Josie back and started to enter her missionary style.

"No, Red, I want you to do me doggie," Josie said, rolling over onto her stomach and getting up on all fours.

Red couldn't help but smile again. He loved fucking Josie doggie style. He loved watching her leaning in to him and grabbing the sheets. He began fucking her hard from the get go. Thrusting deeply into her, she moaned with every stroke.

"Really fuck me hard, Red. I need it," she moaned.

Red really started pumping her then, grabbing her hips and pulling her back onto him with each thrust. Josie came after only a few seconds of this. After shuddering for a few seconds she got into a groove where she was really bucking into him hard. Red had never felt so good fucking a girl.

"I wish you had two dicks, Red. I would love to be sucking a cock right now," Josie said breathily. Since hearing about Red's dream, she was turned on more than ever. Especially since she knew that he loved hearing her talk like that. Red had a hard time fighting back the cum after her comment.

Red was really pounding her when all of a sudden, the bedroom door burst open.

It was Sister Gwen.

"Brother Red, I'm sorry to interrupt…" She looked at Josie whose eyes had almost rolled back into her head with ecstasy and winked. "…but you're not gonna believe what they're talking about on TV."

She flicked on the TV before he had a chance to answer.

Red slowed down to a slower pace as he watched the breaking news about the "perverted pastor" as they were now calling him. He watched with a slight revulsion as the Rev. Simon Pure blustered about his moral depravity.

"Well," Red sighed as he continued to slowly fuck Josie. "I guess the cat's out of the bag."

"So, what are we gonna do, Brother Red? What about the Church? This is gonna kill it," she said nervously. She fidgeted from leg to leg as Josie stared her squarely in the eye as she was being fucked. Sister Gwen was getting wet fast.

"I don't know what to do, Gwen. I really don't," Red said.

Sister Gwen couldn't keep her attention off Josie. Her eyes were almost glazed over in lust as she nodded to Red.

"Well, I know what Sister Gwen can do," Josie said, pushing hard against Red. "She can get her clothes off and come over here and join us."

Sister Gwen smiled. "That sounds like a pretty good plan."

She quickly slipped out of her skirt and top and got on the bed with them. Red pumped Josie even harder as she pulled Sister Gwen over to her and began to lick her already wet pussy. Sister Gwen moaned in ecstasy as Josie's experienced lips and fingers explored her. Josie came again as Red picked up the pace and fucked her with wild abandon.

"Let's switch. I want you to fuck her while she eats my pussy," Josie said.

"Great idea!" Sister Gwen said. "I love Red's big cock."

The girls switched out and soon he was pounding Sister Gwen and slapping her ass while she ate Josie's pussy. Sister Gwen came fast from the fucking because Josie had already gotten her heated up. Josie came again from the cunnilingus.

After a bit, Red pulled out. "Girls, I just can't take it anymore."

"Well, don't waste it!" Josie said and started sucking his dick. Sister Gwen got down and helped her with it. After a few seconds, Red squirted a big thick load all over the both of them. They licked each other's faces clean and then shared a kiss.

As they all sat around afterwards, smoking cigarettes. Red told Sister Gwen all about him and Josie.

"That's so great! I just wish all this other stuff hadn't happened."

"I know," Red said.

"So, Red, what can you do?" Josie said. "Do you think that you can deny it?"

"I don't think so. I mean if they've got the pictures…"

"But what I want to know is how can they even have the pictures…?" Sister Gwen said.

Just then the sound of helicopters became overwhelming.

"What's that?" Sister Gwen said and jumped off the bed. She ran over to the window and looked out.

"It's a helicopter and it's…"

"It's filming you!" Josie cried and pointed at the television. Sure enough, there on the news was Sister Gwen looking out of the window nude. Her breasts and pubic hair were blurred but there she was.

Red got up and looked out the window. He appeared on TV too. As naked as a jaybird. He took a look around his property.

"There are reporters everywhere," he said softly. News crews were parked all up and down his street. He walked back to the bed and lay down beside Josie.

"I'm screwed," he said. "I'll never preach again."

Josie shook her head and began to cry.

"Don't say that, Red. You're too good a person for that. You help too many people."

Sister Gwen came over and joined them.

"Yeah, Red, Josie's right. You can't give up. There's got to be a way."

Red shook his head.

"If I had stolen from my congregation like Simon Asshole Pure, they wouldn't even care. But let me have a little sex and it's the end of the world."

"I would just like to know who did this to you," Sister Gwen said. "You've never hurt anybody."

"Maybe I deserve it," Red said. "For living one way and acting another."

"Nobody deserves this," Josie said. "If I could just get my hands on the person who did this…"

"No, Josie, we shouldn't wish this person harm. I'm sure they had their reasons," Red said. "I just wish they would have come to me first and maybe we could have worked something out."

21

"We did good, baby," Gunter said as he took a bite of his club sandwich. "You got your revenge and a little money for your pain and suffering."

Brother Farlin sat directly across from him. While he had ordered a cheeseburger and fries, he found that he wasn't really that hungry. In fact, he hadn't been hungry since the news hit.

"I can't believe that I listened to you. Red was my friend and I betrayed him because of you. Who are you anyway? You're nothing to me." Brother Farlin hung his head in his hands. "I wish I was dead."

Gunter chuckled. "It's ok, baby. You're just forgetting that that he's the guy who wasn't sharing his pussy with you. He didn't look out for your needs. He deserved it, keeping all that sweet pussy to himself."

Brother Farlin nervously lit up a cigarette. "But that's not really true. I did get laid sometimes. It's just…" He tried to ash the cigarette and only managed to break it in the process. "…oh, I don't know! I'm such a fool!" He put his head in his hands again.

Gunter rolled his eyes. "You've got to grow some balls, baby. Especially, if you're going to go on the talk shows and talk about what a pervert that guy is. You don't want to miss out on that kind of money."

"Talk shows?" Brother Farlin looked up.

"Oh, yes, baby. I've already booked you on several." Gunter smiled back. He had big plans for Brother Farlin. He would do the talk show circuit, next the lecture circuit, then the religious circuit and then the high school circuit. He would not only be able to get his Audi fixed with the money that would be rolling in, he would also be able to buy several new ones as well. This was one of the best ideas that he had ever had.

"You? Wha…?"

"Oh, I'm your manager, now, baby. I hope you don't mind. I just thought that you would want to…how you say…make hay while the sun is shining."

Brother Farlin emphatically shook his head. "I don't want any of this. I wish I had never met you."

"Well, you did, so let's make the most of it."

Brother Farlin narrowed his eyes at Gunter. "And Brother Red is not a pervert. Not any more so than you, anyway."

"Well, what is he then, baby?"

"He's my friend."

"Was your friend, baby. Now, he's your cash cow."

Brother Farlin sat there for a moment. He lit another cigarette.

"No, this is gonna stop."

A worried look crossed Gunter's face. "Don't do something stupid now. This is a going to be a good thing for the both of us. Let's make lemonade out of this lemon, okay, baby?"

Brother Farlin shook his head slowly.

"No, we're not." He looked up at Gunter. "I'm sorry if I said anything mean to you, about being a foreigner and all. I know you can't help it."

"That's okay. I am a foreigner. I admit it," Gunter said and smiled, though it was hard because he could see all his dreams rapidly going down the drain.

"And I'm sorry for saying that I wish that I had never met you. You can't help the way you are. Brother Red says that there's room for everybody. We just have to open our hearts enough so they'll fit."

Now, it was Gunter's turn to shake his head. "No, baby…"

"Yes, Gunter. I'm going to Brother Red and ask for forgiveness. I know I don't deserve it, but I can't let everything that man has done for me slide down the tubes."

"But what has he done for you, lately?" Gunter said harshly, almost spitting across the table. He couldn't understand how Brother Farlin could be so stupid. How he could just throw away all this money? But he also realized that maybe money wasn't everything to a guy like Brother Farlin. It hurt his stomach to even think this.

"Goodbye, Gunter. You're welcome to come with me if you want."

Gunter stared at him.

"Brother Red is a very forgiving person."

For the first time, Gunter began to feel a twinge of guilt. "No, I can't. I have to get my Audi out of the shop."

22

"**M**an, we came as soon as we heard," Brother Abernathy said as he greeted Red, Josie and Sister Gwen at the door of the Cardboard Cathedral. They had had a hard time fighting their way through the crowd of reporters and protesters. Many of the protesters were followers of Rev. Pure. They held up signs up with slogans such as, "Go back to hell, you Demon!" and "Pornography Kills." One of the signs that especially pained Red was one that attacked Josie. It said, "Preachers don't date sluts!"

While he was happy that Josie was indeed a slut, his interpretation of the word was something far different than what they meant. They spit at him and grabbed at him as had made his way through the mob. Red was lucky that he hadn't been torn apart.

Brother Abernathy's clothes were disheveled and looked like they had just been thrown on. Red took a look at the three half-dressed Thai hookers lounging around the reception area and realized the reason behind Brother Abernathy's appearance.

"Thanks, Brother," Red said shaking his hand. He was happy to see that Brother Abernathy was still on his side. It was good to see that it hadn't been him that had betrayed him.

Just then Brother Myrtlewood burst out of the TV production area.

"Brother Red, I've got everything set up. Whenever you're ready to tell your side of the story, we're ready. We can break into our regular programming and start broadcasting it immediately."

Brother Myrtlewood looked in a similar state of disarray as Brother Abernathy. He also smelled heavily of liquor and marijuana. His pants were also still unzipped and his semi hard penis was hanging out. Marcy walked out of the production area a couple of seconds after him, wiping her mouth. It was obvious that he hadn't been the one who had betrayed him either.

Marcy walked over and gave Josie a big hug.

"Thanks, Brother Myrtlewood. Just give me a minute."

Red turned to Josie. "I'm sorry that you had to get dragged into this."

"I'm just glad that I'm here to help you through it," Josie said.

"So, what are you gonna do, Red? Deny it? I'm sure we can say the pics are fakes or something," Brother Myrtlewood said and lit up a cigarette.

Red shook his head. "No, I said that I'm not gonna do that. I can't lie about this. I've been lying for so long about this stuff. I'm tired of it. I don't feel anything is wrong with it. If I lie about or apologize for what I've done, then it'll be like I feel that it's wrong."

"You know that this is gonna kill your ministry, don't you?" Brother Abernathy said, barely unable to keep his eyes off Josie's hot little body.

"Probably. But I've got to stand up for what I believe in. This is something I've got to do."

Suddenly a commotion erupted behind them, at the door of the church.

"You pervert! Let go of our daughter!"

"Daddy!" Josie said as she saw her parents along with Bob and Jenny entering the building.

Hal and Bob rushed over to Red. Brother Abernathy tried to stop them but they pushed him aside. Before he knew it, Hal had knocked Red down to the ground.

"How dare you try to brainwash my little girl, you red headed woodpecker!"

"Hal, leave some for me," Bob said rolling up his sleeves.

"I'll show you what's happenin' now, you son of a bitch!" Hal said as he jumped on top of Red and punched him in the jaw.

"Bob!" Josie cried. "Please Daddy! Stop! Mom! You've got to make him stop! He's hurting Red!"

Priscilla walked over and put her arms around Josie.

"It's okay, Josie. It's normal for you to feel empathy for the man who brainwashed you," she said soothingly. She turned to Marcy. "I hope you haven't joined this cult, too."

"But it's not a cult!" Josie protested.

"Sure it is, dear. It's a cult run by a pervert." Priscilla took a look at Red who was still being held down by Hal. He was sitting on him and lecturing him about how he shouldn't be brainwashing impressionable young girls as a prelude to beating him. She could see the imprint of Red's gigantic penis through his pants and felt a little twinge. "I can easily see why a girl would get...overwhelmed by his..."

"But he's not a pervert! And it's not a cult! He's a swinger and he helps people. Daddy can't hurt him because I love him!"

Priscilla let go of Josie.

"He's a..."

"He's a swinger, Mom. You know, he has sex with people. He's just like me, except he doesn't get paid for it. He never told anybody about it because he was afraid that people would stop supporting his church and he wouldn't be able to help anybody."

Priscilla's jaw dropped. She looked over at Jenny who was also dumbstruck.

"Hal! Bob! Come over here! You've got to hear this!"

Hal looked over his shoulder.

"I'm kinda in the middle of something here," Hal protested.

"He's a swinger," Jenny said.

Hal looked at Red and then looked at Priscilla who nodded her head. He got up off Red and walked over to Josie and Priscilla. Red stood up and dusted himself off. He rubbed his chin where Hal had socked him.

"So, he's a…"

"Yes, Daddy, he's a swinger, You know…"

"Honey, we know what swingers are." Hal looked at Priscilla and nodded her head slightly.

"Honey, there's something we need to tell you…" Hal said and took her hand.

Josie's jaw dropped as Hal told her all about how he and Priscilla were swingers and how Bob and Jenny were also swingers. He told her about their parties and conventions. Josie was stunned, but it did clear up a lot of things for her. For example, she had never understood how her parents could meet so many people and why they were always going to so many parties. And here she had thought that Mom and Dad were just a couple of squares. She was definitely going to have to rethink how she viewed them.

After he was finished, Hal had a few questions for her. "So, is everybody here…"

"I know Sister Gwen is and I think Brother Abernathy and Brother Myrtlewood are too. I don't know about Brother Farlin…"

"Brother Farlin!" Sister Gwen said and snapped her fingers. "I knew we were missing someone. I wonder what happened to him?"

"I think I know," Red said quietly. "He was the one."

"He was the one what?" Bob said.

"He was the one who betrayed me," Red said.

It was like a light was turned on in the minds of everyone there. They all knew beyond a shadow of doubt that he was right.

"But why?" Marcy said. "I thought…"

"I don't know. I just don't know," Red said.

They stood there for a little bit talking and exchanging apologies. Hal couldn't stop telling Red that he was sorry. Now that he knew the truth, he was actually happy that she was dating him. So was Priscilla. She was glad that her daughter had found a lover with such a big cock. She also couldn't help but eye Brother Abernathy's sizable schlong as well.

Finally, Red took a look at the TV production area. "Brother Myrtlewood, it's time."

"What's he gonna do?" Priscilla asked Josie.

"He's gonna go on TV and tell everybody the truth."

Red, Brother Myrtlewood and Brother Abernathy turned and started walking towards the studio. This was it. There would be no going back after this.

"Brother Red! Wait!" A voice yelled from behind them.

They all turned. It was Brother Farlin and Gunter.

"We're sorry. We want to help," Gunter stammered as he nervously walked towards them. His guilt was obvious to everyone.

"But why, Gunter?" Josie said. "Why did you do it?"

Gunter shrugged. "I guess I wasn't listening to the medicine man."

Red looked at Brother Farlin who was as white as a sheet and so jittery that he couldn't stop fidgeting. Brother Abernathy walked over to him and punched him hard in the stomach. He crumpled like a dollar bill.

"I think you two had best be leaving."

Red ran over to them and pushed Brother Abernathy away.

"Stop it!" Red bent down and helped Brother Farlin up. He looked at Brother Abernathy sternly. "You know that there's room for everyone in this church."

Brother Farlin immediately began to weep. Gunter just wanted to fall through the floor.

"Brother Red, we're ready," Brother Myrtlewood said as he leaned out of the studio.

23

"**F**uck her like you mean it!" Red said as Brother Abernathy shoved his big black cock deep into Josie's already stretched pussy.

Josie bit her lip as Brother Abernathy fucked her hard, doggie style. She moaned sharply with each thrust and gripped the sheets tightly. At the same time, she slurped up Brother Myrtlewood's cock and swallowed his pre-cum. Red was finding it hard to focus on her completely because he, in turn was fucking Marcy doggie style.

"Farlin, move in closer and get a shot of her face. I just love the way she looks when she's getting it hard."

Sister Gwen stood on the side watching and fingering herself to yet another massive orgasm. It was amazing how little things had changed since the news reports had come out. After all, here they were, at the Church, fucking their brains out, but now, they didn't care if anybody found out about them. Controversy was one of the most important tools *The Church of What's Happenin' Now* had its disposal when it came to spreading the good news.

Of course things had been a little dark there for a while immediately after Red had gone on the air telling the world about how he was a swinger and how he had just wanted to help people. He had told about his personal beliefs and apologized for acting one way and doing another. He had explained that he had only done this because he didn't expect people to understand and he didn't want to do anything to hurt the people he was most trying to help. He had told them how he was going to keep the church open and that the ministry was going to keep going as well. He said that his purpose in life was to help people and he was going to persevere even if he only had one person sitting in the congregation.

All the staff jumped ship except for Brother Abernathy, Brother Myrtlewood, Sister Gwen and Brother Farlin. It was only natural that people left the congregation in droves, as well, but some did stay. The ones who truly wanted to help people weren't bothered by the fact that their pastor was a sexually active man.

However, these people were in the minority. The attendance really dwindled and there, for a while, it looked like Red was going to have to start selling the church's assets just to keep the charities going. He was on the verge of deciding to make the decision to sell the TV station, but then, just as he began to make rounds of the talk show circuit, a funny thing started happening. People started attending the church again. It was a completely different group of people than the ones who had attended before. These people were open minded and had been moved to hear him speak about his mission and how his church was for people without hang-ups. But moreover, because he didn't believe in judging people for what they did in their personal lives, but rather what they failed to do in regards to their fellow man. Maybe his congregation wasn't as big as it once was, but this time it was a lot more sincere. But perhaps, the real reason was that the church was now really about *What's Happenin' Now*.

Of course, with this new audience, Red realized that he could actually include his thoughts on sex in his messages. They were a big hit and it was then that Josie got the idea that Red should take his sex-positive message on the talkshow circuit. She knew that they would be a big hit. Her relationship with Red had only gotten stronger through the turmoil.

Of course, she and Marcy kept their film careers outside the church going as well. Things were going so great that Josie was finally able to join Marcy as a *Solid Gold Medallion* contract girl. In fact, they were even able to get many people in the industry behind the church. They supported Red by making donations to the charities and helping him with his fundraisers. Even Gunter, whom Red had forgiven, was an active campaigner.

Red also easily forgave Brother Farlin for his betrayal. Especially after he realized that the aftermath of what had happened was really the best thing for him. He had to be honest with the world and more especially with himself. He was a swinger, plain and simple. Why should he hide something like that from the world? Didn't swingers need role models just like everybody else?

Another plus was that Red's writers block was gone and he was finally able to write the book he had always dreamed of, *The Man Who Could Shit Worlds*. It had been a bestseller for weeks, mostly due to his notoriety. Red was already half through the second draft of the follow up piece, *The Man Who Could Shit Gold*. He certainly wasn't any one trick pony, he would assure people of that.

Hal had even started working with the ministry, using his skills as a motivational speaker and self-help guru to give lectures and seminars on behalf of the church. He spoke to swingers groups and other sex friendly organizations.

Red moaned as Marcy bucked against him. That was another thing. Marcy was extremely satisfied since she had finally started sampling Red's big cock. There was no way she was going to stray from the fold now. Josie was a quivering mass as she fucked Brother Abernathy. He was stroking her hard and Brother Myrtlewood was thrusting his penis deep into her throat. After a minute, he changed his rhythm and Red could tell that he was shooting his load. Josie took a big swallow then began to concentrate on Brother Abernathy who was fucking her like a machine. Red picked up the pace on Marcy and couldn't resist slapping her on the ass as he banged her. She squealed and shuddered a bit as she came. He was amazed that he was able to keep from cumming himself. He looked at Sister Gwen over on the side fingering herself. Brother Farlin was going around snapping pictures and jerking off at the same time. Sister Gwen would give him a little suck now and again, just to give herself a little boost. She was too busy playing with herself to give him too much attention. Brother Abernathy then pulled out and shot a gigantic load into Josie's eager mouth, squirting so much that she had to swallow twice. Red then realized that he wasn't going to be able to take it any more.

"Fill me up!" Marcy said.

Red pumped her pussy full of his juice. He rammed it hard, thrusting it as deep as he could go. After he was done, Sister Gwen crawled in bed and began to lick the cum out of Marcy's pussy.

Red just stood there staring. He then began to smile. He went over to Josie and gave her a big hug.

"Everything happens for a reason doesn't it?" He said.

"I guess that's why you had that dream," Josie said as she reached out and began to play with his penis.

"I guess so," Red said.

Josie turned serious for a minute. Something had been troubling her for months and she knew that she was going to have to bring it up eventually. Now seemed as good a time as any.

"Red, there's one thing we're gonna have to discuss."

"What's that?" Red said with a small sense of dread. He hoped that it wasn't anything serious.

"I know you like the black bra and panties, but I don't like wearing underwear. Can you see my dilemma?"

Red looked at her for a minute and then started laughing.

"Are you gonna still like me if I stop wearing them all the time?" Josie said a little nervously.

Red just kept laughing.

"I think I can manage," he said.